G000145807

Also by the Author

EXCHANGE for MURDER

SCANNER

for

MURDER

by

Marilyn Goode

INFINITY
PUBLISHING

All rights reserved. No part of this book shall be reproduced or transmitted in any form or by any means, electronic, mechanical, magnetic, photographic including photocopying, recording or by any information storage and retrieval system, without prior written permission of the publisher. No patent liability is assumed with respect to the use of the information contained herein. Although every precaution has been taken in the preparation of this book, the publisher and author assume no responsibility for errors or omissions. Neither is any liability assumed for damages resulting from the use of the information contained herein.

Copyright © 2010 by Marilyn Goode

ISBN 0-7414-6035-1

Printed in the United States of America

This is a work of fiction. Names, characters, places, and incidents either are the product of the author's imagination or are used fictitiously. Any resemblance to actual events or locales or persons, living or dead, is entirely coincidental.

Published December 2010

INFINITY PUBLISHING
1094 New DeHaven Street, Suite 100
West Conshohocken, PA 19428-2713
Toll-free (877) BUY BOOK
Local Phone (610) 941-9999
Fax (610) 941-9959
Info@buybooksontheweb.com
www.buybooksontheweb.com

CHAPTER 1

Upstate South Carolina, 1994

The car crawled to the side of the road and died. Its only occupant, a young woman, peered frantically through the windshield but her vision could not penetrate the thick blanket of darkness smothering the vehicle. The car headlights were dead and its dashboard a blackout. She opened her door and stared down at the ground. She could see she was far enough off the road as to not be struck from the rear by another car.

"Thank God I made it off the highway." The sound of her voice instilled confidence and quieted her jangled nerves. She continued aloud, "Hate to think what could've happened if I didn't. I'll call Triple A and have them tow me into Moultrie."

She pulled over the square bag containing her new '94 Bell Atlantic/Motorola cellular mobile and carry phone with battery pack and punched in the AAA memory emergency code. It was for this very reason that she purchased the portable phone and now she was very glad she did. The friendly answering voice perked up her spirits. She gave the operator the necessary information and her approximate location being fairly well familiar with the road.

"We will contact the garage in Moultrie and request a tow truck to pick you up. Just stay where you are until they arrive."

The flame from her lighter momentarily brightened the interior of her car as she lit up, sucked in a lung full of cigarette smoke and relaxed. She drew hard with each successive puff until there was only a stub. Crushing it out in the ashtray, she immediately fumbled for another and was

1

about to light it when oncoming headlights caught her eye. Fearfully, she watched the vehicle slow down, drive past, then turn about and pull in behind her crippled car. Bright headlights bore through her rear widow making it impossible to recognize the vehicle or its driver. A dark shape loomed past the truck's glaring high-beams and someone rapped on her car window.

"Miz Talbot, they sent me to carry you back to Moultrie. The tow truck is out on another call. Didn't want you sittin' out here by yourself."

Recognizing the voice, she unlocked her door and opened it. A worrisome load lifted from her shoulders.

"That was thoughtful of them. I was afraid I'd be spending the night out here." She slipped out of the car. "Should I leave the key?"

"Yes, ma'am, you'll have to. Leave it on top of the visor and don't push down the door locks."

Amelia Talbot slid the car keys atop the visor, picked up her purse and phone bag and slammed the car door shut.

She slung the double carry straps over her shoulder and felt his hand take her elbow to steady her as she stumbled along the uneven shoulder of the road. She saw that his vehicle was a pickup truck.

He assisted her up into the high truck cab, went around and climbed in on the driver's side. The engine roared to life and he drove out onto the highway in the direction of Moultrie.

Wishing to break the silence, she said "Were you around the station when Triple A called?"

"Yes ma'am. Was just killin' time so I offered to come get ya."

Amelia pushed back her short blonde hair. "I'm glad you did, it was so dark there." A tremble swept over her body.

The driver made a sharp turn off the highway onto a rutted dirt road.

"Hey! Where are you going?" Her loud demand was clipped off as fear clutched her throat. She fumbled for the door handle.

The truck stopped short and one strong hand grabbed a handful of her hair and pulled her toward him.

"Get back here! I thought we'd have a little party before I took you into Moultrie."

Her body flushed hot with the rush of adrenaline. "Are you crazy? I wouldn't have anything to do with you, you pig." She clawed at his face, feeling warm sticky fluid under her fingernails.

He shot a short jab to her jaw which left her groggy. Darkness enveloped her and she realized the headlights were shut off. He pulled her past the steering wheel and her legs bounced down the truck's step. He dragged her away from the vehicle and dropped her upon the rough weedy ground.

"I won't tell a soul," Amelia pleaded, "just let me go. Please let me go."

"You know ya been asking for it, with all your 'Good mornings' and 'How are you today?' I could smell you were fresh from the shower. I wanted to grab you and lick your cunt."

His huge hands pawed her body, tearing at her clothing. In the dim light from the door courtesy lamp Amelia struggled to fight off the man, begging him to leave her alone.

It was no use. Cool air chilled her exposed skin. Her breasts, her waist, and down. All she could hear was his raspy heavy breathing. He held her down with one hand while the other undid his belt and unzipped his pant's fly. His knees pushed between her leg and he fell upon her. A stab of pain filled her as his erection probed then plunged. Her scream was cut short by the clamp of his hand over her mouth. He rode her body to a climax. His back arched with the ejaculation.

Tears slid into her ears and she twisted and turned her face away from the stubble of his chin and the smell of his foul breath. Muffled sobs coughed up in her throat. He slapped her hard across the face but her mind refused to acknowledge the physical abuse and his violation. She rocked her head from side to side as he withdrew from her.

A rough, calloused hand clutched her breast, pinching its nipple until she cried out. He hit her again.

"I tol' ya to shut up."

He sucked at her breast while his fingers painfully explored between her legs which brought another cry from her.

"Please let me go, please," she begged, struggling to get the words out of her mouth. His powerful forearm was pressed hard against her throat making it difficult for her to talk.

He got up onto his knees and, by a handful of her hair, yanked her to a sitting position. One hand grabbed her upper jaw, the other, her lower. She grabbed his wrists and tried to break his hold.

"Bet you ain't ever had it this way."

Gaping wide in his vice-like grip his resurrected penis was plunged deep into her mouth, gagging her. Humping back and forth, he achieved a second climax deep in her throat. With breath cut off, Amelia Talbot fought to stay conscious. Bile rose into her mouth as he withdrew. She turned her head to the side and vomited.

In the dim glow of the door courtesy lamp she saw the glint of the thick-bladed knife. It looked like a hunting knife. He waved it in front of her face. Its serrated edge reminded her of shark's teeth. She stared up into the dark sockets of the man's wild, glistening eyes and read death. Her death.

"Dear God," she began praying.

The blade flashed crosswise and was the last thing Amelia Talbot comprehended in this life. It cut through the jugular vein and carotid artery, inflicting severe damage to the thyroid cartilage, releasing a spout of blood. The murderer held the head so the chin rested on her chest avoiding most of the spurting blood. She died a slow death.

His smile grew into a light chuckle. "That'll teach you to sashay your ass around town."

He rose to his feet, tucked himself into his pants and zipped up. He lowered the truck tailgate and unfolded a tarpaulin, spreading it out on the truck bed. He went back to Amelia Talbot's body, lifted her with ease, and laid it upon the canvas. Hopping up onto the bed, he pulled the body into the center of the covering, wrapped it carefully so the wind would not lift the edges, and rolled it to the front of the truck bed.

He slammed the tailgate shut, marched back to the driver's door, climbed in and drove off toward the lake.

* * * * *

The town of Moultrie, South Carolina housed its municipal offices in a typical ante-bellum white-columned building across the town square from a similar structure housing the Moultrie County Courthouse. In the days of "King Cotton" the county was exceedingly prosperous. Large wooden hotels had been built to house "drummers" who traveled with their sample cases from manufacturers in the capital city of Columbia. Today, the old wooden buildings housed an art gallery, a tea room, and the Chamber of Commerce. Some stores were family-owned and had been in continuous operation since before the war; the Civil War.

The county did not have much in population but was beginning to feel the tentacles of business and bedroom communities reaching from the nearest city. The town, with its quiet refinement, cushioned itself about a center square where the Confederate Soldier's monument was prominently displayed. Residents took pride in the town's architectural gingerbread and curlicues corbels and cornices. Window drapes of deep claret velvet, trimmed in gold tassels, hung from the rods inside the Baxter-Lewis House, a bed-and-breakfast inn that contributed the right touch of elegance to the town's ambience.

Moultrie was in the heart of the Bible belt. Strong Judeo-Christian beliefs and principles wove through the fabric of traditions and customs of all its citizens. Citizens of strong opinions and persuasions.

5

Flags, both the Stars-and-Stripes and Stars and Bars billowed from the halyards in front of the courthouse announcing the town of Moultrie was open for business.

A twinge of repugnance swept through Laura Crowder as she slowly drove her Mercedes around the town square of Moultrie, South Carolina and slipped into an angled parking space facing the center of the square. She was agitated and tired. It had taken a total of seven and a half hours to drive down to Moultrie, with a motel night in Charlotte, North Carolina. She had timed her arrival to be during business hours.

Her eyes swept the buildings. "God, how I would hate to live in this backwater town," she mumbled. A quick glance at the store signs lining the opposite side of the square caused her to shake her head. "There isn't even a decent place to shop. I can't imagine what on earth possessed Mom and Dad to come to this God-forsaken place to retire."

Laura picked up her attaché case and purse, slid out of the leather seat and locked the car. She stopped an approaching woman and asked directions to the Bank of Moultrie. Following the given information she proceeded down the narrow side street, turned and entered the bank's marble lobby.

Inquiring about lock boxes, the young teller, whose name tag said Sandra Perkins, directed Laura to a woman sitting at a desk in the rear. Laura introduced herself and asked about the safety deposit box in her parents' names. The clerk checked her card file.

"Yes, Philip and Judith Crowder have a lock box here, number 1072, and your name and signature are on the card which gives you access to the box in the event of their death."

"My parents were killed two weeks ago. I have been notified by a Mr. Butler Brown to come down and have their wills probated. I'm assuming the wills are in the lock box."

The woman slowly nodded her head. "Yes, I remember now. It was a shock to hear about their accident." Then, straightening her shoulders, asked, "Do you have some identification with you?"

"I brought my birth certificate and my business license." She opened her attaché case and presented the papers to the clerk.

"Until you have the wills probated I am not allowed to permit you to remove any other items from the vault box except the wills of your parents."

"I understand."

"When you probate the wills then the contents of the box may be removed at any time by the executor or executrix of the estate, which I assume will be you."

"Since I am their only child I would presume that I am."

"Please sign the record card."

Laura did so, then together, they entered the vault room and, with two keys; one, Laura's, which had been sent to her last year by her father, and the other, the clerk's, they opened the lock box and Laura removed the wills.

"Please take them to the clerk of the circuit court and have them probated."

"Thank you for your help. I'll be back sometime before I leave Moultrie to pick up the rest of the contents."

Laura's heels clicked over the brick patterned street and up the granite steps of the courthouse. The small sign hanging from the L-bracket above the doorjamb read *Clerk of Court*. She entered the office and lightly tapped the chrome summons bell.

"I'll be right there," came the slightly agitated woman's voice from the depths of the records room.

Laura braced herself to confront whom she believed would be an aging tyrant who ruled over any person or lawyer trespassing in her domain. "They're all alike," she grumbled. "Think they're guardians and preservers of the county's historical well-being."

A young red-haired woman, about 45, strode out of the records room. Her dark green suit was streaked with dust and her hair disarranged.

"I'm sorry it took me so long. I was in the midst of moving some of our oldest record books back where they belong. We just had them put on microfilm." She slapped at the dust on her skirt then walked over to the counter separating herself from Laura. "I'm Marylee Carson, the Clerk. How may I help you?"

Laura was pleasantly surprised by the woman's friendly manner.

"My name is Laura Crowder. I'm here to have the wills of my parents, Philip and Judith Crowder, probated."

"Oh, yes," her voice dropped to a softer tone. "I'm so sorry. Please, won't you come in." She reached over and opened the gate to the inner office. "Did you bring the wills?"

"Yes, I just came from the bank."

Marylee Carson unfolded the notarized self-proved wills and quickly scanned them for the name of the appointed executor. Laura presented the same identification as she did at the bank. The clerk examined them and nodded.

"I'll have the certification papers ready in no time, Miss Crowder. As soon as I sign these you can collect the remaining contents of your parents' safety deposit box. I'll make you copies of the wills for your personal files. The originals I'll keep to be recorded."

"Yes, I understand."

"How many copies of your qualification do you think you'll need?"

"I really don't know. For now, I'll take five for each estate, and if I need more I'll come back."

The redhead nodded. "Fine. That'll be fifty dollars."

"Must be a universal price. That's the same as it is in Richmond."

"Oh? I really don't know. Our costs are set by the state."

"That figures," Laura said, mockingly. "Will you take my check?"

"Of course, Miss Crowder, and I would suggest you open estate checking accounts as soon as possible so that you can keep the proper records for the Commissioner of Accounts. He's a crotchety old man and a stickler for proper records."

Laura couldn't help but smile. "Got one of them, too?"

Marylee Carson lifted her eyebrows questioningly.

Laura explained. "It's just that it seems the courthouses are run by stereotype characters all over our country."

A slight flush covered the clerk's face.

Laura quickly corrected herself. "All except you, Miss Carson. I was expecting a much older woman to be Clerk of the Court."

The slender redhead straightened back her shoulders. "If you had come two weeks ago you wouldn't have been wrong. Our clerk, Mrs. Burshog, just retired. She is seventy-three."

Incredulously, Laura stared into the clerk's dark eyes then saw the woman's lips twitch at the corners into a smile. The humor hit them both and they burst out laughing.

Marylee Carson picked up a tissue, dabbed at her eyes, and said, "I saw from your business license that you are a lawyer, with whom do you practice?"

"I'm with the firm of Katz, Katz and Katz in Richmond, Virginia."

"Sounds like a lot of cats. Any kittens?"

Laura chuckled. "No. That's K-A-T-Z."

The clerk laughed. "Sorry, but I just couldn't resist saying that."

"It's okay." Laura leaned over the desk toward the young woman. "Would you happen to know a Butler Brown, attorney?"

"Oh, yes. Mr. Brown is in the building next door." She indicated the direction with a tilt of her head." His office is on the second floor."

* * * * *

Laura was ushered into Butler Brown's office by his secretary. Momentarily, she was repulsed by the man behind the over-sized oak desk. He resembled a ponderous mound of face and body. Laura caught her revulsion before it registered on her face. With confident stride, she crossed the room and held out her hand. The man pushed himself from the chair with an agility belying his weight and firmly shook her hand.

"I'm Laura Crowder, daughter of Philip and Judith Crowder."

"A pleasure to meet you, Miss Crowder." He dropped back into his chair causing the heavy wooden piece to squeak. "Please be seated." He waved her to a leather armchair.

Laura sat and removed the copies of her parents' wills from her attaché case. "I note you prepared the wills."

"Yes, I did. Terrible tragedy. You have my sincerest sympathy."

She pushed down the sorrow swelling in her chest and watched the obese lawyer open his desk and withdraw an envelope.

"These are spare keys to your parents' home and car. Your father had them made, to be held by me, in case of an emergency. When you returned my call, telling me you were coming, I got them out of my safe to give you. I took the liberty of having Philip's car picked up from the airport and delivered to the house. It's in the garage."

"That was very thoughtful of you. Saves me a lot of time." She took the offered envelope. "I already have keys. Dad sent them along with the key to the safety deposit box. I just qualified as executrix of both estates. I was wondering who you might suggest I get to give me an appraisal of the house, land and furnishings. I don't intend to stay very long. I have to get back to Richmond."

"Have you been out to the place, yet?"

A feeling of guilt pricked her conscience. "No, I haven't. In fact, I've never been to or seen the place since they moved down from Richmond."

The contemptuous look on the fat man's face kindled an angry reaction in her gut. It also inflamed the smoldering coal of guilt she carried since being informed of her parents' untimely and wrongful deaths.

"You know how it is, just so busy." Her trembling voice belied her words.

He nodded condescendingly. "Yes, yes, I know. Never enough time." His watery eyes swept over her legs. "Do you plan to stay at your parents', I mean *your* house while you stay in Moultrie?"

"I imagine so." Then smugly added, "I didn't see any suitable hotel or motel on my way in."

"Oh yes. There is the Hilltop Motel just out of town on Highway 57, and there's two bed and breakfast inns. I always recommend the Baxter-Lewis House, myself. Lots of atmosphere."

Laura sniffed. "I'm sure, but first, I'd like to check out the *homeplace*, so to speak."

"Don't blame you. I'm sure you'll find it very comfortable."

"Can you tell me how to get there?"

"Go out Highway 57, that's the main drag through town," he indicated, with a wave of his hand, a westerly direction, "about five miles passed the Hilltop Motel. It'll be on your right just after you pass the gates to ERIN. Yours will be the next driveway."

"ERIN?"

"Your property adjoins that of ERIN. The owner is Patrick Ryan."

She nodded, stood and extended her hand. The mountain of flesh quickly rose. "I'll be in touch, Mr. Brown." She released his hand, turned on her heel and left, closing the door behind her.

* * * * *

At the Moultrie Bank, Laura went through the lock box, listing the contents on the inventory sheet. There didn't seem to be anything of great importance in the box, just some insurance policies, and birth certificates of her parents. There were some stocks and bonds but she expected more. She wondered where the rest was. She came across a legal size envelope, opened it and found a smaller envelope marked "To be read in the event of the death of Philip Crowder." Also enclosed was a key. Her throat tightened as she became overwhelmed with her guilt. She would read it when she got home. *Home.* She thought it was an unusual word for her to think.

She closed the lid of the lock box, summoned the vault clerk, and they both reinserted the box into the vault and locked it with both keys.

* * * * *

The Mercedes glided smoothly along the roadway. Laura caught a glimpse of the stone columns guarding the gateway to ERIN and slowed the car so as not to miss the next road to her parents' home. As she approached the turn-off she saw her father's handiwork. An avid gardener, he had landscaped the entrance with azaleas and camellias. It was mid-April. The azaleas were in full bloom.

Laura stopped the car to fully appreciate the beautiful sight. A strangling lump tightened her throat and she swallowed hard to get rid of it. Gunning the car's motor, she moved quickly along the driveway. Her first view of the house made her feel as if a huge hand had clutched tightly about her heart. It was just what her mother always said she would build. It was a two story grey stone house, much like those seen in the valleys of Pennsylvania,, with the addition of two symmetrical ells. Solid and strong, it nestled down into the foundation plantings of azaleas, yews, and boxwood.

Laura shut off the engine and sat quietly, admiring the beauty of the house. The tightness about her heart relaxed. Taking her purse and keys, she got out, cast a wary eye about, then locked the car.

Before the imposing structure Laura felt small and terribly guilty. Guilty for not coming down. Guilty for giving all sorts of reasons as to why she couldn't.

So many times Mom called and I kept giving her excuses.

When unlocked, the heavy wooden door easily swung open and Laura stepped into a room-size foyer. Square slabs of polished gray granite covered the floor and a rust and black Persian rug commanded attention to the center. In the center of the rug was an ornately carved oblong mahogany table. The flower arrangement had long since withered. Its dried petals lay strewn upon the table top. Laura walked over and rested her hand upon the fine wood. A thin film of dust covered the surface. She stroked the table, remembering it from earlier years. It had always held a place of prominence in their Richmond home. Moving to one side of the table, she brushed over an area. The scar she had made years ago, overturning a bottle of nail polish remover, was still evident. She ran her finger over it, lightly tracing the marred spot.

"Don't worry, a little mayonnaise will fix that."

She could still hear her mother's voice, but the blemish was still there. She walked through the lower rooms admiring the arrangement and décor. All of her parents' furniture fit nicely into the rooms. Fine Queen Anne furniture. Not true antiques, but solid mahogany pieces made by the country's finest furniture makers. Beautiful replicas of a bygone day. She remembered every piece and wistfully touched each as she passed. The furnishings flooded her with memories of when she was growing up in Richmond. St. Catherine's school, University or Richmond, and T.C.Williams School of Law.

Slowly, with heavy heart, she climbed the stairs to the upper level. The master bedroom and bath were just as her parents left it on that fateful day. In the dressing room, her mother's nightgown and robe had been hung in a hasty manner. Her hand slid over the silkiness of the gown.

Why were they in such a hurry? If only they had missed the plane. If only they had changed their minds about going.

Laura stroked the gown gently, envisioning her mother. *If only.*

Clutching the nightgown, Laura ripped it off the hanger and threw the garment on the floor. Her teeth gnashed, her hands clenched into fists, and her body filled with anger. Anger for her loss. Never to see her parents again. Anger at herself for not coming down to visit. She wanted to tear the garment into shreds. She stared down at the shimmering material then slowly bent, picked it up, and cradled the nightgown in her arms. Blunt realization bludgeoned her denial and the truth shattered her heart. The finality of death and the numbness of complete loss swallowed her. Losing all control, Laura dropped down upon the vanity bench and loosed anguished, pent-up wails. She wrapped her arms about herself and rocked back and forth in tortured grief. She finally reconciled herself to the deaths of her beloved parents.

A long while later, she went down stairs and got her suitcase from the car.

She settled in the room her mother chose for her. It held the same bedroom furnishings. The same diplomas on the wall. All her old belongings. The closet held pieces of clothing she kept at their home in Richmond, anticipating her infrequent visits. Her schedule had been too busy—too taken up with her new law practice. Her apartment. Her friends.

A deep shuddering sob racked her body. She shook her head and said aloud, "I have to stop thinking about it. I can't change what happened. But, oh God, if I only could."

She unpacked and hung up the few pieces of clothing she brought. The more she moved the more tired she became. The long day's trip, the stress of probate, her ponderous grief took their toll. When the last item was put in place she lay across the bed and fell asleep.

CHAPTER 2

Last night, after her shower, Laura had checked the contents of the refrigerator and found only a half-carton of eggs and a small block of cheddar cheese along with the usual jars of condiments. A loaf of bread was in the freezer so she had made herself a cheese omelet with toast for supper. Today, she would inquire in town about a grocery store or some place where she could buy a few food items.

The drive back into Moultrie didn't seem as long as driving out yesterday. It was close to eleven o'clock when she parked in one of the angled parking spaces around the town square.

Perhaps I'll take a few minutes and walk around the square and go through some of the shops. There's got to be something here that endeared my parents to this town.

Laura got out, locked the car and stood on one of the crosswalks that ran through the park-like square. Her eyes were drawn to the obelisk in the center. Walking toward it, she read the inscription on the Confederate monument. A reminder of their sacrifice to a lost way of life. Six park benches offered a respite under the wide spread of live oak limbs but, this morning, the only takers were pigeons. Slowly, she turned and took in the panoramic view of Moultrie.

The town square was surrounded by old buildings that oozed an aura of quiet refinement that she didn't feel yesterday. Two large houses of Victorian architecture sat across from each other. Both were bed and breakfast inns. The small sign on one read Baxter-Lewis House. Wine colored drapes trimmed with gold tassels hung at its windows. Her curiosity piqued.

Perhaps someday, I'll go in and see what it looks like. What am I saying. I won't be spending much time in this town.

Two ante-bellum white-columned buildings anchored each end of the square. Moultrie County Courthouse was chiseled in the granite lintel of one. The other was marked County Administration Building. She was surprised she hadn't noticed the beauty of the courthouse when she climbed the stone steps the day before looking for the clerk of court

Guess my mind was on other things.

She crossed the herringbone patterned brick paved street and strolled along the sidewalk, close to the store fronts. Tourists milled about, cameras hanging from their necks and shopping bags bulging with purchases. She had forgotten the town was hyped as an historical place. From the looks of it business was good.

She lingered long over the exquisite display of diamonds in the jewelry shop, and wondered who, in this small town, could afford such pieces. Then slowly, she migrated into CAPER'S.

Tripped chimes announced her entrance as Laura opened the door to the dress shop. A stunning woman, possibly in her late forties, lifted her head and removed her glasses. Her blonde-grey hair was swept back in a French twist and Laura immediately noticed the woman's elegant designer suit. The woman came forward and held out her hand.

"I'm Caper Morgan, the owner of the shop."

Laura was taken back by the hospitable manner in which she was greeted. It took a moment for her to recover and extend her hand.

"I'm Laura Crowder."

The two women shook hands and the older woman peered intently into Laura's face.

"Crowder? Are you related to Philip and Judith Crowder?"

"My parents." A tightness clutched her throat when she felt the woman's hand tighten upon hers. Laura quickly shook off the sorrow. "You knew my parents?"

"Judith was a customer and a friend of mine, and they were also members of Moultrie County Club." Caper took a step back and gave Laura a scrutinizing look. "Yes, I can see the family resemblance. You have Judith's eyes." She moved forward and put her arm about Laura and said softly, "I guess you're down to handle the estates."

Laura felt an immediate closeness with this stranger.

She knew Mom. She must have seen her just before she and Dad left on their trip. "Yes, I had the wills probated yesterday."

"Staying out at the house?" Caper asked.

"Yes."

"A beautiful place."

"Yes, it is."

The woman propelled Laura toward the racks.

"Please, take your time and examine my line of clothing. I think you'll find it as good as anything in Richmond."

Laura pulled up short. "How did you know I was from Richmond?"

"Laura, if you don't mind me calling you Laura, I told you that Judith and I were friends. She spoke of you often. She was very proud of you."

A stabbing pain shot through Laura and she clutched the edge of the display case.

"Are you okay?" A troubled look filled Caper Morgan's eyes. "I know this must be very hard for you."

"Yes, yes, it is but I'm okay." Laura straightened.

"I want you to know that if there's anything I can do to help you while you're down here, please do not hesitate to ask."

Laura gave Caper a weak smile. "Thanks so much."

The shopkeeper moved toward the racks and slipped the hangers, looking at each garment. "How long will you be in Moultrie?"

17

"I haven't decided. I guess it will depend upon how long it will take to get an appraisal of the house, land and furnishings."

Caper spun about. "You plan to sell the house?"

"That's my thoughts at this time. I just don't know what to do."

Caper pat Laura's shoulder. "Don't do anything hasty. You have a beautiful estate there." Then turning about, she removed a garment from the rack and held it up in front of her. "I would say this would be your style and color."

Laura couldn't hide her surprise. The dress was indeed what she would have chosen and the color was perfect.

"If you have a few minutes, why don't you try this on. I'd like to see it on you."

Laura drew back, thinking it had to have an astronomical price, then slowly accepted the dress and was pointed toward the dressing room.

It slid over her slender form with sensuous ease. The bright green silk illuminated her hazel eyes, heightening them to a shade she rarely saw. A quick flip lifted her thick black hair over the back neckline and her hands smoothed the dress close to her body. She took a peek at the price tag and swallowed hard. Prices like Montaldo's in Richmond, even though Montaldo's was facing Chapter 11 bankruptcy. It was the finest upscale clothing store in Richmond and she regretted its future demise.

When she stepped out of the cubicle, Caper Morgan couldn't hide her pleasure. "Yes. It suits you, all right. I really appreciate your trying it on so I could see how it looks."

In the dressing room, Laura removed the garment, placed it back on the hanger and redressed.

Handing it to the shop owner, she said, "It's a gorgeous dress. Perhaps, before I leave Moultrie, I'll stop by again."

"I certainly hope so." Caper slipped the garment back on the rack. "Do you think you'll be going over to the club before you leave?"

"The club?"

"Moultrie Country Club."

"Oh! Well, I really don't know. I don't think I'll have any reason to go."

"Maybe you will," Caper said and extended her hand again.

This time Laura was quick to respond. "It was a pleasure meeting you, Mrs. Morgan."

"Please call me Caper." She gave Laura's hand a gently squeeze. "I'll be in touch."

Outside, walking along, Laura felt a warm glow of friendship. She liked Caper Morgan. *She could be a true friend.* A glance at her watch told her it was a few minutes past noon. Maybe she'd find a place to have lunch before she looked for a grocery store.

She entered George's Sandwich Shop, sniffed the aroma of grilling hamburgers, and waited to be seated. It seemed all the tables were occupied. Tourists and office workers was her guess. The waitresses were scurrying about taking orders or delivering them. She was about to turn and leave when she felt someone take hold her hand. She looked down at a petite blonde with sparkling blue eyes.

"You can share my table, if ya don't mind?"

Laura was impressed by her kindness.

"I would like that very much."

The young woman fairly bounced with enthusiasm. She held out her hand. "I'm Sue Bader."

Laura took the young woman's hand. "I'm Laura Crowder," and she received a firm handshake.

"I work for Bruce Pierce, he's the county planning commissioner. Are you new around here?"

Laura hesitated. She didn't want to go into a long detailed discussion as to why she was in Moultrie. Her hesitation was picked up by the young blonde.

"I guess I ask too many questions. It's really none of my business."

"No, that's all right. It's just that it's a painful subject."

Looking questioningly at Laura, Sue said, "I think I just made the connection. Are you the daughter of Philip and Judith Crowder?"

"How did you know my parents?"

"As nice a folks as they are--or were, most all the people in Moultrie knew them. As I say, I work for the planning commission. Your dad was a volunteer on the beautification committee and has worked with us on several projects. He was a fine gentleman."

"Yes, he was, Thank you." Laura bit her lip to hold back the tears.

The waitress took her order and she settled back to study the interior of the sandwich shop.

It seemed an old establishment. Faded prints trotted along the shop wall. Victorian ladies riding sidesaddle on skinny-legged horses. Women of fashion, snobbishly posing under parasols, riding in horse-drawn carriages. Somehow, the faded prints or the dingy wall coloring did not detract from the quiet sedateness of the eatery. Laura nodded with approval.

"It's not too bad," her table companion said.

Her attention was brought back to the young woman.

"I think it's rather nice."

"Used to be Millie's special place for lunch. Millie is my dearest and closest friend, but she lives in Harrisonburg, Virginia, now."

"Really! I'm from Richmond."

A spark of life glinted in Sue Bader's eyes. "Her husband's a reporter for the *Harrisonburg Blade*. Name's Bob Sutherland. Have you ever heard of him?"

"No, I'm afraid not. I get the *Richmond Times-Dispatch*."

The waitress set the salad plate and glass of iced tea before Laura and went about her business.

Laura noticed that Sue Bader had finished her lunch and had settled back in her chair.

"For a small town, like Moultrie, seems there's a lot happening," the petite blonde remarked.

Laura dabbed her napkin to her mouth. "What do you mean?"

"When Millie and I were working on the timeshare exchange murder cases, the killer actually came down to Moultrie and murdered Wendy Schrum, one of the waitresses that worked here." Seeing Laura's surprised reaction, Sue continued, "He was really looking for Millie--to kill her."

"My God! Did you say you were working on a murder case?"

"Yeah, but that's another story. Perhaps, sometime, we can have lunch and I'll tell you about it. It's also how I came from Cleveland, Ohio, to live in Moultrie, South Carolina." She paused, then added, "And now we have another mystery. One of the women from town is missing. Amelia Talbot. Word has it her car broke down about four miles east of Moultrie and she called Triple A on her mobile phone. Triple A contacted the Milford Garage here in Moultrie. When the tow truck got there, the car was unlocked and the key was on the visor but she was nowhere around. She just disappeared. No trace of her."

A shiver ran through Laura. "Poor thing. What could have happened to her?"

"Don't know. Police are still working on it, but from what I hear they have no leads."

"That's terrible."

Sue Bader gathered up her purse. "Gotta run, now." The young blonde stood. "If you need any help call me, Sue Bader, at the planning commission. Your dad was a fine man and I do want to say how sorry I am about your parents."

Laura nodded, her throat tightened making it unable for her to answer.

The young woman placed her hand upon Laura's shoulder, gave it a little squeeze, then left.

A calmness came over Laura as she sat and gazed out the window upon the town square. She watched Sue Bader cross the center park and enter the administration building.

Laura unconsciously nodded. *For the few years Mom and Dad spent here in Moultrie, I'm sure they enjoyed them. The people are so friendly and caring.* She paid the bill, asked about a grocery store and received directions.

At the bank, she opened checking accounts for the handling of her parents' estate matters, then she crossed the square, slid into her car's leather seat, and headed out of town to find the grocery store.

On the outskirts of Moultrie she entered the parking area of a large shopping plaza with a well known supermarket. It was another unexpected surprise. Walking the aisles she couldn't help but notice the store was every bit as upscale as Ukrops in Richmond. Purchases made, she packed them into her car and drove back to the house. As she came through the door she heard the phone ringing.

"Miss Crowder, this is Butler Brown. I have asked our county appraiser to get in touch with you. His name is Clifford Morris."

* * * * *

He parked his pick-up truck at the front door and got out. Slender, with a wiry frame, he had the right body for the jeans, boots and denim jacket he wore. Hitching up his pants, he looked about the grounds and house with a keen appreciative eye. To Laura, who was peering out the sidelight of the front door, she thought he didn't fit the picture of an appraiser. Yet, he surely must be. She wasn't expecting anyone else. He approached the front door and Laura opened it. Removing his western style hat, he held out his hand and she placed hers in his.

"Cliff Morris." His eyes took in the foyer. "Mr. Brown said you were interested in having the land, house and furnishings appraised." He dropped Laura's hand. "Plan to sell everything?"

Her doubtful look sent his eyebrows skyward.

"Changed your mind?"

"No." She tended to drag out the "no", sounding more doubtful.

"Well, let me leave my card. I get paid by the hour and I have someone I call in to appraise furniture." Looking about again, he added, "And I can see I'll need him for this job. You have some fine pieces here." His eyes took in the full bonnet highboy standing along one wall of the foyer, flanked by two Chippendale chairs.

"Yes. My mother liked fine furniture."

"My hourly charge is fifty dollars, and the furniture appraiser gets the same. We're very thorough, quick, and we do a good job. Also run auctions in case you might be interested in holding one." He pushed a card into Laura's hand. "Beautiful place you got here. Shouldn't have any trouble selling. Just give me a call when you feel you're ready. We can take it from there."

He had a brusque, ingratiating way about him, but Laura decided, when letting him out the door, that if and when she needed those services she would call him.

He climbed into his pick-up truck, adjusted the wide brimmed felt hat, and drove out to the county road.

Now, why didn't I let him set a date to appraise the place and the furniture?

She went back into the kitchen and made a fresh pot of coffee. While it brewed she took inventory of the pantry items and found it fairly well stocked. It was obvious her parents did not expect to be away for any length of time. The dying flower arrangement on the foyer table attested to that. Had her mother planned to be away long she would have removed it.

The door chimes startled Laura. She went to the door and peeked out the side light. A tall black woman, middle-aged, hair pulled back in a tight bun, straight, patrician nose and wide set eyes, stood waiting. Laura pulled open the door.

"I hope I'm not interrupting you, Miss Crowder, but I thought I'd come to catch you while you were home. My name is Lizzy—Lizzy Macon, I'm the housekeeper."

"The housekeeper?"

"Yes, ma'am. I work for your mother. Clean the house once every two weeks. Today is the day I usually come but since I heard about what happened..." she cut off and dropped her head, "I mean about your Momma and Daddy being killed in that plane crash..."

Laura reached out and took the woman's hand, guided her inside and closed the door.

"Lizzy, if this is your regular day for doing the housekeeping then please go ahead. I did notice there was dust on the foyer table. When was the last time you cleaned?"

"Just before your parents left for their two week vacation." Realizing what she said she stammered, "I mean..."

"I understand Lizzy." Laura looked about and thought this woman probably knows more about where things are in this house than I do. "How long does it take you to clean the house?"

She was taking off her coat and heading for the kitchen. "It usually takes me about five hours. Your momma always went and had her hair done."

Laura watched her go into the utility room, pull out a hose, wand, and vacuum head, and turned to go into the living room. "I usually start upstairs, if that's all right?"

"Oh, yes. Do your usual routine. But where is the vacuum tank?"

"This is the vacuum. Your mama has a central vacuum system. This is the connection. The tank is in the garage."

Oh, brother, am I smart. "I've never seen one before."

"Come and I'll show you how it works," Lizzy said smiling.

Laura followed the woman into the living room and watched as she bent down, lifted a cap covering a wall opening and plugged the connection into the socket, flicked the switch, and the vacuum whispered into action. There was hardly any noise, just a sniffing sound.

"That's the first time I saw that kind of a vacuum. Pretty nifty."

"And very good. There's a connection in every room and in the hallways."

"I wont keep you from your work, Lizzy. I'll be in my father's office if you need me." Laura turned to leave.

"That's the only room I don't clean. Your father's orders."

"I understand, Lizzy. He is, I mean, he was pretty particular about his papers and things." Laura felt her throat tighten and turned.

"Miss Crowder, if you need or want something, just give me a call upstairs and I'll help you."

Laura could hear the softness in the woman's voice and knew she meant well. She sniffled, nodded to the woman, and entered her father's office.

CHAPTER 3

Laura put her breakfast dishes in the dishwasher and glanced out the window above the sink. The view was of a hilly meadow, dotted with wild buttercups and daisies that seemed to beckon her. She decided to take a walk.

Opening her closet, she pulled out a pair of her old blue jeans and stepped into them. They were just a bit snug about her hips. An oversized University of Richmond sweat shirt hung loosely about her, hiding the tight fit. She slipped into her old sneakers, tied them, and went out the patio door.

A glance around the patio revealed a set of classic aluminum outdoor furniture, a concrete bench, and a covered gas grill. If she planned to stay for awhile she thought she might hunt up the chair cushions. They would probably be in the garage.

The sweet smell of daisy and buttercup pollen filled her nostrils. A heady fragrance of summer. She knew these fresh, aromatic, open field scents could not be found on downtown Franklin or Jefferson streets in Richmond. Carefully, she picked her way through the field, not venturing too far, and turned to look back at the house.

The opening line from DuMurier's *Rebecca* popped into mind. Something like "*Last night I dreamt I went to Manderley again.*" Perhaps not the exact words, but just what she felt as she studied the grey stone structure with the long, wide rear patio and the two wings that balanced the design. Laura hugged herself and thought how much her mother must have loved this house. How proud she must have been and eager to show it off. *The many times Mom called and asked me to come down. The excuses I gave her for not being able to come.* Laura's stomach gave a lurch and she started walking back to the house.

The sound of tall grass being whipped and the deep hacking of heavy panting stirred a sense of fear and she turned and met the eyes of a huge yellow dog bounding toward her. Its tongue lolling out the side of its mouth displaying sharp canine teeth. Laura screamed, threw her arm across her face and fell to the ground awaiting the dreaded onslaught. Petrified, she remained stiff and still. The cold nose pushed in against her cheek and she screamed again.

"Blarney, no!"

The command was gruff and authoritative. Laura felt two strong hands lift her from the ground and turn her about. She clung to the muscular arms as she sought to see the whereabouts of the vicious animal.

"Blarney won't hurt you."

It was a strong male voice and Laura looked up into a pair of steel grey eyes. Her breath suspended. She became oblivious to everything except his eyes. They were compelling. Magnetic. She felt naked. As if he could see into her very soul. A wisp of dark hair fretted in the breeze over the man's frowning, concerned look. She read the momentary flicker of recognition that registered within the grey pools as they swept over her face. His strong arms released her and he stepped back. Gently he picked a piece of dried grass from her hair. Laura felt tongue-tied and embarrassed. She moved back from the strong aura of the tall masculine figure and, looking down, brushed at her clothing. *Oh, Lord, look how I'm dressed.* Her old clothes looked disreputable. Silently, she chastised herself for being weak and insipid, stood tall and squared her shoulders.

"I'm terribly sorry my dog frightened you." His voice apologetic.

"A vicious, attacking animal like that should be on a leash," she snapped.

"Vicious? Blarney isn't vicious."

The huge golden dog was running circles around them and the man gave another command.

"Blarney, sit!"

The dog obeyed instantly.

Laura admitted to herself that the animal was well trained. Perhaps she did get the wrong impression when she saw it bounding through the grass toward her. She studied the dog. Its bluish tongue hung out the side of its mouth giving it a fierce look, but its eyes seemed to be creased in a grin.

Do dogs smile?

"Maybe I was a bit hysterical. I've been very upset lately."

She tried to turn and her legs felt like rubber. She would have dropped to the ground had the stranger not picked her up bodily and carried her toward the house, much against her loud protests. She was cradled against his chest and could hear the deep thumping of his heart. A strong steady thump, while hers raced within her chest. The fingers of his right hand pressed into her thigh while the fingertips of the other pushed against the curve of her breast, generating an erratic heart beat and intense internal heat. She squirmed away from his pressing fingertips.

"Stop squirming. I'll set you down when I get to the patio."

Laura simmered with his rebuke and remained tense as his long strides brought them to the patio. He placed her on her feet next to a concrete bench and she sank down upon the cool seating.

"I'm Patrick Ryan, your next door neighbor. You must be Laura, Philip's daughter."

Again she was surprised. She stared up into his grey eyes.

"You knew my father?" Her voice caught in her throat.

"Of course I knew him, after all, we've been neighbors for three years. He was a fine man. He worked on the Moultrie beautification committee, and we worked on many projects together through the county council. Please permit me to extend my deepest sympathy in the loss of your parents." He studied her face. "Are you feeling any better?"

Laura pulled herself upright. "Of course I am. I really don't know what came over me."

"Too much grief and too much burden," he half whispered. "I didn't know you were here otherwise I would have asked your permission to walk the back fields of your property. Phillip had given me permission but now I should ask for your permission."

The big golden retriever plopped down upon the cool concrete of the shadowed patio, its sides heaving with each pant. The tall dark haired neighbor moved to the side of the patio, turned on the spigot, and the dog jumped up and lapped at the water. It was an action well practiced.

"You've been here before?"

"Many times. Inside and out."

"Oh? Then you knew my parents well."

He looked at her with surprise. "Of course. They were an exceptional couple. You look very much like your mother."

Laura felt the tightening in her throat and pushed back her building tears.

"Thank you." She straightened up, pushing back her shoulders. "I'm down to have their wills probated and try to settle the estates."

"Then are you going back to Richmond?"

Her mouth opened in surprise. "You do know a lot about me, don't you?"

"I know you're a lawyer and live in Richmond." His smoky grey eyes slid over her figure. "You must have a tough time holding your own in the courtroom."

His insinuating remark fanned her anger and her reply was sharp.

"What makes you say that?"

"People have a tendency to distrust beautiful women," his eyebrow cocked with his appraising smile, "and you certainly are beautiful."

She felt her cheeks flush. This stranger was causing a storm of conflicting emotions which she disliked, and his remark, though half flattering, was patronizing.

"Not at all!" Her chin jutted proudly. "The courtroom is a place for facts--facts which are prudently sifted and weighed by judge and jury. I don't believe any physical appearance on my part would prejudice my cases."

A slight waver in her voice belied her statement. Before any court engagement she chose her clothes with care, depending upon which judge presided. A suit well tailored, with its severity softened by a scarf. She knew some judges looked with disdain upon female attorneys. She also had advised young felons to cut their long hair, shave off their beards and wear presentable clothing, not jeans, to court if they wanted to help their case.

"Spoken like a true counselor."

The deep mellow voice held a touch of mockery but his handsome face broke into a pleasant smile which stirred sensations of tickling feathers in the pit of her stomach. Her physical reaction appalled her. Her body was reacting as if it were sex-starved. *Well, wasn't it?*

"And, pray tell me, Mr. Ryan, what do you do for a living?"

The tall man shifted his posture and gazed out over the field. "I have several kinds of businesses."

Thinking of the small town her voice held an edge of sarcasm.

"Oh? And what kinds of businesses might they be?"

He brought the full impact of a steady steel gray gaze upon her as he responded.

"Local and international."

The tingling feathers flew into a flurry in the pit of her stomach. She tamped down the feeling and was about to sneer a disparaging remark when he continued.

"Mostly international. I'm in the diamond business, and have several other investments."

Laura's chin dropped before she could catch herself. She was aghast that, with such investments, he lived in this backwater town of Moultrie, South Carolina.

"How on earth do you keep up with your business ventures living in this small out-of-the-way place?"

He shook his head with disbelief and drilled his cool grey stare directly into her eyes.

"I'm sure you've heard of computers, on-line, internet, fax and international phone service." His eyes mocked her. "I can conduct most my business from my home. Once in awhile I travel to Amsterdam, but most of the time I go to New York."

"Is that where you came from originally? I seem to detect a slight northern accent."

"Yes, but I never realized I had a northern accent. Is it that obvious?"

"No, as a matter of fact you have a very nice voice." *Now, why in the hell did I say that?*

"That's very kind of you to say." He pulled himself erect. "I have to be going, but if there is anything I can help you with as to settling your parents' estates please don't hesitate to call me."

"Thank you, but I think I can handle it."

"I see! An independent and resourceful woman."

"I try to be. And yes, Mr. Ryan, you do have my permission to walk the back fields–with Blarney."

He nodded, gave a short whistle, and strode briskly away with the golden dog racing ahead then stopping to wait for its master.

Laura pushed up from the bench and went into the house, glancing once over her shoulder at the retreating figure.

That afternoon, in her father's study, she was examining her parents' personal papers and insurance policies. It was time to open her father's letter from the bank box.

She picked up the small envelope, slit the top with the letter opener, and read.

To my beloved wife, Judith, or my loving daughter, Laura:

It breaks my heart to write this but I must. My darling Judith, had you predeceased me I would have torn this letter up and told you, Laura, face-to-face.

Do you remember in 1964 when VEPCO got permission from DuPont to send me down to South Carolina, outside of

North Augusta, to the atomic plant on the Savannah River? I was sent there to observe some reactor's electrical generating capacity. Met some local guys and we went out for a few drinks. I met this young lady, Hazel Harris, whose husband was in the Navy. She was a very nice person and we spent several evenings together. One thing led to another and I am confessing to having an affair with her.

When I returned to Richmond I kept in touch with her. She informed me that she was pregnant. I knew the child was mine as she was not a promiscuous person. It was not her nature. A son was born in 1965 and she named him Peter. When her husband's ship came back from the Gulf of Tonkin he divorced her. Hazel went back to Moultrie, her hometown. Through the years I did my best to support and help educate the child. Hazel was killed in 1988 when a drunken driver hit her head-on when she was on her way to work . At that time Peter was 23, out of college and working in Moultrie.

When I contemplated early retirement I convinced you, Judith, to visit Moultrie. You fell in love with the town, its people, and the tract of land we looked at and then bought all of which is now yours, Judith, or perhaps it's Laura. In either case, the property is free and clear of any debts and I have left substantial investments and insurance to carry you through the years.

However, in the bank lockbox you found a key. This key is to a strongbox that is in the garage above my workbench. The contents are stocks and bonds I would like to leave to Peter and I would greatly appreciate you honoring my wishes as my last gift to him. He is a fine young man and I have had the pleasure of working side-by-side with him. He never knew I was his father.

Please don't hate me, Judith. I love you very much. I could not bear to see the hurt in your eyes if I told you. Try to remember me in the same way you have in the past. I love you dearly. Always did and always will

Your loving husband,
Phillip

Laura was both shocked and sad but relieved that her mother never knew about the indiscretion. She was crushed to know that somewhere in this town of Moultrie, South Carolina she had a half-brother. She picked up the key and went into the garage. As Butler Brown, the attorney, had said, her father's car was in its place. She looked about on the shelving and found the strongbox. Opening it she found the rest of the stocks and bonds she expected to find in the bank lockbox. There was also an insurance policy with the face value of Five Hundred Thousand Dollars and the beneficiary named was Peter Harris. She brought the strongbox into the house, set it on her father's desk and plopped down into his office chair. Tears over-flowed and, with all the pent up emotion of loss, of denial, and plain self-pity she bawled like a baby. She let it all out, sniveled loudly, then wiped her eyes and face. She suddenly felt very tired.

The phone rang.

"Laura, this is Caper Morgan. I was wondering if you would have dinner with me this evening at the club." She hurried on hearing the short intake of breath. "Generally, I eat alone, but I would like to have you join me, or did you have other plans?"

The lovely face of the shopkeeper came into mind as Laura said, "I'm really not up to it. I just got some very distressing information." Then quickly added, "I just can't seem to get myself together."

"Then I think you need to relax a bit."

Laura thought Caper might be right. "What time and where is the club?"

"About seven-thirty, and I'll come by to pick you up."

"I hate to put you to any trouble. I can drive there."

"Not this time. Maybe next. I'll be by at seven-thirty."

"I'll be ready." She hung up the phone.

What on earth am I going to wear? She thought of the shimmering green silk dress Caper had her try on. If only.

She set aside the papers and went up stairs to shower.

Later, wrapped in her father's voluminous terry cloth robe, Laura curled up on the living room sofa, reading. The chimes of the front doorbell startled her. She clutched the thick robe about her as she glanced through the door's sidelight.

A young, neatly dressed black man stood on the porch with a parcel tucked under his arm. He grinned at her and she felt her embarrassment warm her face. She quickly opened the door.

"Miz Crowder, Miz Morgan sent this over to you." He shoved the box into Laura's hands then briskly strode back to his pickup truck.

Dumbfounded, Laura watched the retreating vehicle, then glanced down at the elegant box with the flowing inscription of Caper's. Setting it on the foyer table, she hurriedly opened it, half knowing what it contained. The silken gleam of the green dress softened her eyes and she pulled it from the box and pressed the garment to her cheek, relishing the feel of the expensive fabric. A small card slipped to the floor. Laura picked it up and read it.

WEAR THIS TONIGHT. I'LL EXPLAIN LATER.

CAPER

Laura shook her head and went upstairs to find a pair of her mother's shoes that would be appropriate with the simple, elegant dress. She and her mother had worn the same shoe size since her high school days.

CHAPTER 4

When Laura opened the front door, Caper Morgan swirled into the foyer, grinning from ear to ear. She studied Laura.

"You look sensational."

"Thank you, but I expect to pay for the dress."

"No you won't. Your mother paid for it."

Astonished, Laura waited for further explanation.

Caper took Laura's hand. "My dear, just before your mother left on her trip she ordered a dress for this fall. The order came in, but... I hung the dress in my stock and since the prices were fairly comparable I took the liberty of sending you this in exchange for your mother's order. I hope you don't mind."

Laura's heart flooded with warmth. She brushed her hand down the shimmering fabric and half-whispered, "I guess I could consider it her last gift to me."

"I would say so," replied Caper, then pushing Laura toward the door, said, "Let's go and enjoy the evening."

* * * * *

Moultrie Country Club was an elegant antebellum structure. It smelled of old money and new. The huge marble floored foyer was flanked by two parlors furnished with eighteenth century English pieces. A round polished mahogany table in the center of the foyer reflected an arrangement of fresh flowers; rubrum lilies, velvety white callas, and dark red bird of paradise. Green ivy trailed from the vase and stretched onto the table. It was an impressive arrangement.

Caper took Laura in tow and led her to the entrance to the dining room.

The somberly dressed maitre d' gave a slight bow as Caper approached him. Laura noticed his eyes swept over the proprietress appreciatively.

"Good evening, Mrs. Morgan."

"Good evening, Edmond. How are you?"

"Very fine, Mrs. Morgan. Thank you for asking."

"Edmond, this is Laura Crowder, daughter of Philip and Judith Crowder."

Laura extended her hand. She was impressed by the thin dark haired maitre d' who seemed to effuse the epitome of politeness and efficiency.

Instantly he took Laura's hand in his and with a saddened face, said, "Permit me to offer my most sincere sympathy, Miss Crowder. Your parents were truly very fine people."

As members of this club, Laura realized her parents would have been known to Edmond. She swallowed hard and responded, "Thank you, Edmond."

He pulled two leather clad menus from his stand.

"Is there any place in particular you'd like to sit, Mrs. Morgan?"

"A quiet spot, please, Edmond."

"This way, please."

They followed the tall maitre d' to a table for two next to a set of tall, wide windows overlooking the rear verandah and golf course. There was still enough daylight for Laura to see the long undulating double green behind the clubhouse. Beyond was a spectacular view of a lake that seemed to extend beyond the horizon.

Laura sighed, "What a gorgeous view," as she sat in the chair Edmond offered.

Caper nodded. "Yes, it is."

"The usual, Mrs. Morgan?" Edmond asked.

"Yes, that'll be fine, Edmond." She turned to Laura. "What would you like to have before dinner?"

"Perhaps a glass of white wine would be fine."

The tall dark maitre d' snapped his fingers and a young waitress hurried in response. Slowly, the two servers walked away as Edmond gave the bar order to the waitress then returned to his stand at the entrance to the dining room.

Laura glanced about, admiring the elegant furnishing and tableware.

"This is a lovely clubhouse."

"Yes, it is. I'm sure, since you hold your parents' membership shares, that you will be entitled to enjoy the amenities of the club. I feel certain the board will approve passing the membership on to you."

Laura's eyebrows arched. "You mean I can come here for dinner?"

"Philip and Judith held a full membership, which means you can use all of the facilities of the club. The swimming pool, recreational center, golf course and the clubhouse. I'm sure you'll enjoy coming here, while you're in town."

Her last words reminded Laura that she did not plan to stay in Moultrie. Her plans were to sell her parents' home and furnishings and return to Richmond. *But while I'm here...*

Their drinks were placed before them and Caper lifted her glass.

"This may sound a bit crass, but I'd like to make a toast to Judith and Philip. Your mother was a good friend of mine and I'll miss her very much." She raised her glass. "To you, Judith, and you, too, Philip. God rest your souls."

Tears blurred Laura's eyes. She raised her glass and added, "To you, Mom and Dad. I'll always love you. Please forgive me."

Setting down her glass, Caper asked, "Forgive you for what?" Seeing the hurt look in Laura's eyes, said, "I really don't have any right to ask, but I can't imagine you doing anything that needed your parents' forgiveness. They were extremely proud of you."

Laura swallowed hard. "It's just that they called me so many times to come down and I always had some excuse. Some were legitimate, and some not. I could have driven down here but I just kept putting it off."

Caper reached across the table and patted Laura's hand. "You don't really think they held that against you, do you?"

"I hope not."

"Laura, your Mom and Dad would never have been that petty."

Laura sniffled. "You make me feel so much better by saying that. Thank you, Caper."

Caper Morgan settled back in her chair and opened the menu. "Let's see what they have tonight. I recommend everything. It's all good."

Laura studied the menu for a few minutes. "I think I'll have the broiled scallops."

"Sounds great to me, too."

The waitress appeared the moment the menus were set aside, took their orders and left.

"Have you made up your mind to sell the house?"

"I guess so. Butler Brown sent the county appraiser over yesterday, but I didn't set an appointment to have him appraise the house and furnishings. I don't know what it is but something is holding me back."

"Good! Don't be in such a hurry to sell. Even if you have to go back to Richmond, you can always come down for long weekends and such."

"But it takes a lot of money to maintain two residences."

"True, but I'm sure--and I don't mean to be prying, but I'm sure there will be a monetary settlement in your parents' deaths. After all, the reports say the accident was due to the plane's malfunction. Have you been contacted by the airline as yet?"

"No."

"If I were you I'd check into it. I'm certain there'll be a class action lawsuit between the victims' families and the airline."

"Yes, I'm sure you're right."

"Meanwhile, I would think your parents have put enough aside to run the household, and everything else, for a number of years. Philip struck me as being quite a sensible person and well into investments."

"I've been going over their insurance. I've contacted the companies and I'm ready to send them the policies and copies of mom and dad's death certificates, and my certificates of qualification as executrix."

"Fine! At least you'll have some idea where you stand money-wise."

Their dinners were placed before them and they settled down to enjoy the food.

"I'm really surprised how friendly everyone is here in Moultrie."

"We pride ourselves with our southern hospitality. I think you'll find most of the folks in the county friendly."

"I have so far." Laura told of meeting Sue Bader at George's Sandwich Shop.

"I know her," Caper responded. "She works for Bruce Pierce, the county planning commissioner. Came down from Cleveland, I believe, and a very close friend of Millie Coger. Millie's a Sutherland now. Married a newspaper reporter from Harrisonburg, Virginia."

"Yes, that's what she told me. I guess in a town this small everyone knows everything about everybody."

"You can say that again," Caper chuckled.

Their dishes were removed. They refused desert but ordered coffee. Edmond approached.

"I trust you found everything to your liking?" He was addressing Laura and she beamed under his attentive care.

"It was delicious, Edmond."

"Fine. Now I have been asked to deliver two after-dinner drinks to you ladies. Compliments of a member." He put the liquor menus in their hands.

Laura sat straight and looked about and Caper reached over and pat her hand.

"Not to worry, Laura. Seems you have an admirer and that's great. What will you order?"

She glanced down at the liquor list. "I'll have Frangelico, please."

Edmond nodded, "And you, Mrs. Morgan?"

"A B-and-B, Edmond, thank you."

"I shall bring them after you have your coffee."

The tall somber man slipped away as quietly as he came. The coffee was deep flavored, delicious, and soon gone. Laura looked about the room trying to make eye contact or see a smiling face that would reveal their cheer-giver, but saw none. Everyone seemed to be deeply engrossed with dining or discussion.

Caper smiled. "Don't be too concerned. I'm sure it's a harmless offering. Probably because you're the prettiest woman in the club tonight."

Laura blushed with the compliment. She was certain Edmond overheard as he placed the drinks before them. His lips curved into a slight smile.

The sweet liquor warmed her as it went down, and, for a few more minutes, she and Caper enjoyed the remaining evening. The thought of returning to the emptiness of her parents' house seemed a let-down after experiencing such pleasant dining.

Don't know why I should feel down, I live by myself in Richmond.

* * * * *

From the kitchen window, Laura saw the huge yellow dog romping across the field, followed, with purposeful stride, by his tall handsome master. Ryan's bright red shirt and khaki pants seemed appropriate to Laura for a walk in the fields or for hunting.

Patrick Ryan and his dog, Blarney. He seems to be heading this way. My God, I've got to get into something presentable, and quick.

She took the stairs two at a time, pulled open her closet door and scrambled into a floral print jumpsuit. Hastily, she ran a comb through her hair, applied a light coat of lipstick and dashed down to the lower floor as the door chime sounded. When she opened the front door she was flushed and breathing hard.

Patrick's eyes swept over her.

"You seem out of breath and look feverish. Are you okay?"

Laura squirmed under his scrutiny. "Of course I am. I was just--exercising." Her color deepened with the lie.

Again, his steel grey eyes moved slowly over her breasts, her waist and the curve of her hips. Laura could almost feel them slide over her like a pair of caressing hands. Her body began signaling unexpected messages but she was determined to ignore her physical response to this unsettling, nerve-fraying man. She commanded her eyes away from his and looked into the soft brown eyes of his dog. The dog looked as if he were smiling at her.

"Is that what keeps you in such good shape?"

"Really, Mr. Ryan, I think you're a bit impertinent." To counter his too personal remark, she said, "I see you still have that vicious dog unleashed."

"Blarney is not vicious. Here, let me show you."

He grabbed her hand and instantly a prickling sensation climbed her arm, spreading an erotic desire throughout her body. Her immediate thought was to pull her hand away, but she did not. She could smell an intermingling aroma of aftershave and fresh laundered clothing as he leaned close in against her.

"Hold out your hand, palm up, like this."

He extended her hand then gave a command to the dog. "Come!"

The big golden retriever came close.

"Now, Blarney, say hello to Miss Crowder."

It sniffed then licked Laura's hand and sat on its haunches gazing up into her face.

"He's waiting for you to say something nice to him."

"Oh! Well, er, that's a nice doggy." She hardly recognized her voice, it was squeaky and unsteady, but not from fear. *I wish he'd let go of my hand. No, I don't! What the hell's the matter with me?*

41

The animal's tail thumped hard upon the entry step and, again, Laura thought it was grinning.

Ryan straightened. He was only inches from her. He seemed reluctant to release her hand and when he did, he took a short step backward.

"Miss Crowder, I came over to discuss some business with you. I know your time is limited and I wanted to give you my proposal before you did anything rash with your parents' property."

"Rash? I don't believe I'll be doing anything rash regarding their property."

"I didn't mean to infer you would. I was wondering if we could go inside and discuss it?"

She became flustered when reminded she had not invited him in. Pushing back the heavy wooden door, she waved him to enter.

Without being told, Patrick Ryan went directly into the living room and sat in one of the wing chairs flanking the fireplace. She remembered him saying, and it was quite evident, that he was familiar with her parents' home. She followed and sat upon the sofa facing the fireplace, curling one foot beneath her.

"Have you decided upon a sale price for the house and land?"

There he goes, right to the point. All business. "No, I haven't. The appraiser, Mr. Morris, was here but I haven't set an appointment for him to evaluate the property."

"I happen to know the value of the land per acre and I know there are 15 acres mentioned in the deed."

"I see you did your homework."

"No, not actually. Your parents' land was once a part of the land I own and is mentioned in my deed as an exception therefrom because of the intended sale to Philip and Judith."

"Oh! So I guess you now want it to be joined with the parent property. Is that it?"

"Something like that."

"Since you're so familiar with the land value, and I'm sure you're familiar with the cost of building, I assume you are prepared to make me an offer."

"Yes, I am."

Laura lowered her eyes. A nagging feeling bubbled in her gut. *Is this what Mom and Dad would want me to do? Since they were so friendly with Mr. Ryan, should I consider his offer?*

Laura's hands clenched, knuckles white, and their twisting and wringing did not go unnoticed by Patrick.

"Perhaps I came at an inopportune time. You seem undecided."

"I am undecided. I want to sell, yet...", tears brimmed in her eyes. "I really don't know what to do." Her voice trembled with emotion.

Patrick came over, sat beside her, and took her hand in his. Laura trembled. His aura of virility caused sensuous waves to wash up and down her spine. Here was this drop dead gorgeous hunk of a man sitting beside her, holding her hand, and she really knew nothing about him. For all she knew, he could be the abductor of that stranded woman motorist in the county. Possibly a killer. Laura was completely at his mercy. Alone and vulnerable. A shock of fear swept over her.

Patrick Ryan gave her hand a slight squeeze. "If you'd like, I could come back another time," His voice was soft, reassuring.

"No!" The conviction in her own voice startled her and she clutched his hand tightly. *Why don't I want him to leave?* Laura shook her head and released Patrick's hand. *Guess I'll have to get off the proverbial 'pot' and start settling Mom and Dad's estate. I might just as well find out what his offer is.* "Well, Mr. Ryan, what is your offer? Is it going to be a 'ballpark figure' or firm?"

"Firm. One million dollars, which includes the furnishings."

Laura's head shot up and she stared, incredulously, into the cool grey depths of Patrick's eyes.

Was he joking? Was he making fun of her, trying to see if she knew anything about property values. Was he going to start laughing, knowing the property wasn't worth that amount. Or was it? He did say 'firm'.

Laura's mouth hung open and Patrick lifted her chin with his finger and closed it. His body seemed to gravitate toward her and his eyes locked with hers. She felt certain he was going to kiss her. Reluctantly, she forced her body to back away.

Her body was betraying her. It desired to press closer to the man. She stared at the curve of his lips and wondered how they would feel upon hers. She felt his hands upon her shoulders, fingers pressing hard upon the jumpsuit material. A myriad of emotions flooded her. She shook her head. *I can't have this!*

She thrust her arms outward, breaking his hold, and started making excuses.

"I truly believe, Mr. Ryan, you're trying to take advantage of me."

Ryan lifted his head and laughed.

"Taking advantage of you over what? The price of the property or your beautiful and desirable body?"

"Oh!" Laura sprang to her feet, and Ryan did the same.

Her face burned with incrimination. She did enjoy it. Seeing the storm clouds moving across his eyes, Laura decided it was time to end his visit. And to do so quickly.

Leading the way to the front door, she flippantly said over her shoulder, "I'm sure your proposal price to purchase was intended to make me seem foolish, since I know nothing about the value of the house or land." She was thinking in terms much less than what Ryan quoted. She had seen the property tax evaluation.

Before Laura could open the door, Patrick put his hands on her shoulders, turned her around, and stared directly into her eyes.

"I said my offer was firm and I meant it. I trust you will give it some thought." He quickly pulled her to him and kissed her hard upon the mouth. "That seals my verbal contract."

Laura, dazed by his kiss and bewildered by his monetary offer, clung to the knob of the heavy wooden door. She watched her enigmatic neighbor stride down the side path to the field. The golden dog frolicked along at his heels.

She leaned back against the thick oak door and pondered Patrick Ryan's offer to buy--and his kiss. Was his kiss just to seal the bargain or did he intend more? She was at a loss as to which was the more important. She could still feel the tingling sensation of his lips upon hers.

CHAPTER 5

At lunchtime, Laura walked into George's Sandwich Shop and looked for Sue Bader. She spotted the young secretary and waved. The exuberant blonde grinned and waved for Laura to join her.

"How have you been? I'm so glad to see you're still in town. Do you still plan on selling your parents' place?"

Her questions came fast and Laura smiled into the woman's excited face.

"Hey! Give me a chance to sit down before I answer all those questions."

Laura slipped into the booth across from Sue. The young secretary reached over and pat Laura's hand.

"I'm sorry. I shouldn't ask all those personal questions, but I hope you don't sell. Why don't you stay here in Moultrie?"

"And what would I do about my job in Richmond?"

"Job, blob. You could open your own practice right here in Moultrie. All we have is Butler Brown, and you saw him. We need another attorney."

"That may be true, but I don't think Mr. Brown would think kindly if I did."

"So what! Live and let live, I say. Hey, get a life! Preferably one where you'll be calling the shots." Sue took a bite of her sandwich as Laura gave the waitress her order. Swallowing, she continued. "I happen to know Philip's place, er--I mean *your* place, adjoins Patrick Ryan's." She took a deep breath. "Have you met him yet?"

Laura's heart double thumped at the mention of Patrick's name.

"Yes, I have, and his dog, too."

Sue frowned. "I didn't know Patrick had a dog."

Laura noticed the use of the given name.

"You know him?"

"Slightly. He was more interested in my friend, Millie."

"Oh? Wasn't Millie interested in Patrick Ryan?"

"At first, maybe, but then she met Bob--Bob Sutherland. The guy she married. He's a real sweetheart."

Laura's eyebrows arched. "Did Millie ever say what it was about Ryan that turned her off?"

Sue finished her sandwich, dabbed her lips with her napkin and met Laura's gaze.

"Yeah. She said he didn't seem too polite. Never said thank you. Just gave orders and expected them to be followed."

Probing the recesses of her memory, Laura couldn't ever remember Patrick Ryan saying thank you to her, either. But, then again, she couldn't remember an occasion whereby he would have had the opportunity to say so. She knew he was authoritative. It was in his voice. To her, Ryan seemed a man of few words but lots of action. It was the thought of action that aroused physical feelings and brought a flush to her face.

"He does seem rather abrupt, at times."

The waitress set Laura's order before her, slipped the bill next to her plate and left.

Laura munched on a mouthful of tossed salad as Sue settled back into the cushioned booth and watched her new acquaintance. She waited for an in-between bite.

"What is your opinion of Patrick Ryan?"

Again, arching her eyebrows, Laura looked Sue straight in the eyes.

"I really haven't formed an opinion of the man." Seeing Sue's expectant look, she added, "I only was with him twice. Once, when his dog ran me down, and second, when he made an offer to buy my parents' home."

"He did?" Sue showed surprise.

Laura immediately regretted her words. She knew it could be a matter of minutes and the town would know about Ryan's offer to buy.

Sue, still holding her surprised look, half-whispered, "Did you accept his offer?" Seeing Laura's expressionless face, Sue said, "I guess I shouldn't be asking that, either. None of my business."

Laura lowered her eyes. "It doesn't matter. I haven't accepted his offer. I just don't know if I want to sell or not."

"Now you're talking!" Sue pat Laura's hand. "Take a good look around here before you jump the gun. You just might find Moultrie as wonderful a place to live as I do."

Laura nodded. "I don't plan to be hasty. I've kind of slowed down since I got here. Taking a different perspective."

Sue Bader gave a firm nod. "That's the way to do it." She glanced at her watch. "Gotta run." Looking Laura in the eye, she said, "And don't worry, what you've told me here will not be mentioned by me. Would you mind if I called you sometime--sometime when you're back in Moultrie?"

It was the shy way Sue asked that made her request acceptable.

"Anytime, Sue. I don't know much about the town. Maybe you could show me around."

"Be glad to. How about Saturday?"

Laura chuckled at the spontaneousness of her new acquaintance.

"I guess that would be okay. What time?"

"I'll meet you here at one o'clock. Okay?"

"Sounds fine."

Grinning, and with a slight wave, Sue Bader left the restaurant.

Finishing her salad, Laura wondered if there had been anything between Sue Bader and Patrick Ryan. It seemed she detected a slight trace of hesitancy in Sue's voice. She shrugged, paid her bill and left.

* * * * *

Friday morning the phone rang.

"Hope you don't mind my calling but you did say something about seeing our fair city, and I say that factiously. City, it ain't. You said at one o'clock tomorrow. Is that still on?"

Laura recognized the voice of Sue Bader, the young woman she met in the sandwich shop.

"Oh, I don't know Sue, I don't know if I'm up to it."

"You sound a bit down in the dumps. Are you feeling okay?"

"Yes, it's just that I learned a bit of distressing news."

"There's nothing like fresh air and sunshine to lift the spirits. Believe me, it won't take long. No more that an hour or two. I can pick you up about one or one-thirty, take you for a spin, and have you back home by four o'clock. What say?"

Laura heard the enthusiasm in Sue's voice and didn't have the heart to disappoint her. "Okay. I'll meet you, tomorrow, in front of George's at one."

"I'll be there."

The line went dead.

Laura grimaced and shook her head, *Why did I commit myself to going?*

She walked out to the roadside mail box, pulled down the box door and took out the mail. An edition of the *Moultrie Monitor* was included. It gave Laura an idea.

In her father's study she booted the computer and went on line, did a search for Moultrie, South Carolina to see if the town was even up-to-date with a homepage. It was. She did a search for the *Moultrie Monitor* and the paper's homepage came up. The main news report was the disappearance of Amelia Talbot. Her car was found beside the highway, unoccupied. Her pocketbook was missing. The ignition key was on top of the visor. Searchers were out combing the surrounding area and woods. No clue has been found as yet. Laura felt a chill.

God, even in a small town like this crime prevails.

She clicked on to back editions to1988 and found the accident in which Hazel Harris was killed. A later edition listed her obituary which Laura read. It praised Mrs. Harris's work in the community, her volunteering with the local school for under-privileged children, and her exhaustive work with the church.

"Humph! Those accolades don't change my mind about the woman. I still hate her." She shut the computer down and went upstairs to get into something comfortable. Still chastising herself for accepting Sue Bader's invitation to tour the town, she removed her suit and donned her U of R sweat shirt and a pair of jeans. There wasn't going to be any country club dinner tonight. She planned to fix a salad and heat a can of soup.

The phone rang.

"Damn! Who can that be?"

"I was wondering if you were amenable to having dinner with me tonight?"

Laura recognized the voice immediately. Patrick Ryan.

"I'm really not in the mood for any festivities. I hope you don't mind. Besides, it's such short notice. Almost like an after-thought."

"Actually, it was an after-thought. I was sitting here, mulling over my loneliness and you popped into my mind. It wasn't a planned idea."

At least he's honest. "Well, perhaps another time."

"How about I bring dinner to you?"

"What!" *Is he trying to convince me to sell the place to him? Does he think that little peck on my lips impressed me?*

"I can bring dinner for two to your door. Prime rib, roasted potatoes, carrot casserole. How does that sound?"

Laura's mouth watered. Prime rib. "Really, how do you plan to manage that?"

"I have the best cook in the world, and with Robert's help I can deliver dinner at around seven o'clock. How does that sound?"

She gave it short consideration and said, "I'll fix the salad." *And find out just what you have in mind, Mr. Ryan.*

50

Laura went upstairs to change into something more presentable.

* * * * *

Getting out the good china, Laura set the dining room table, using place mats, and linen napkins rolled in silver napkin rings. Everything was easy to find as her mother stored them exactly as when Laura was young and living at home in Richmond. She put out water goblets and balloon wine glasses, assuming the wine would be red. Then moved the two candlesticks from the buffet and placed them on the table. In the kitchen, she opened the bag of prepared salad greens mix and tossed them in a bowl along with some thinly sliced green onion and a light coating of Italian dressing. She set the bowl on the buffet.

Now she waited for her opportunistic neighbor. It was going to be interesting to figure out Ryan's intention for this soirée.

At seven sharp the doorbell rang. Laura opened it and met the broad smile of extremely white teeth on a very black face.

"Miz Crowder, my name is Robert. I am Mr. Pat's butler and I have brought dinner. May I bring it to the side door?"

"Of course. Please do."

Robert went out to the SUV, drove it around the side entrance to the kitchen and unloaded a huge hamper.

Laura stood in the kitchen and watched the man as he efficiently lifted covered dishes from the basket, as if he had done it a hundred times. He made several trips to the van and with the last trip he was followed in by Patrick Ryan.

"Robert", Patrick Ryan's voice seemed to fill the room, "this is our neighbor, Miss Laura Crowder."

"Very nice to meet you, Miz Crowder, and please accept my sympathy on the loss of your Mama and Daddy."

Laura was taken back by the sympathetic tenor of the butler's voice. "Thank you, Mr. Robert."

"Just Robert, Miz Crowder. Now, if you will leave the fixin's to me, I will be ready to serve in a very short time."

Laura turned and Ryan followed as she led the way into the living room. She watched Ryan settle down and felt a twinge of anxiety, then seated herself at the far end of the sofa. She couldn't help but notice a slight smile curl Ryan's lips.

"I don't bite."

"Maybe not, but I feel more comfortable in my own space."

"I heard that you had your parents' wills probated."

"Lord, news travels fast in a small town."

"Yes, it does, however there is nothing personal to the business of probating wills. They will soon be of record in the Will Book for all to see and read. It's public information."

"Yes, I know. It just surprised me how quickly the news gets about in Moultrie."

"Small town." Patrick stretched out his long legs, crossed them at the ankles, and leaned back into the cushions of the couch.

Laura was surprised how urbane he appeared. His light textured suit fit him well, and his loafers had to be of Italian leather. Yet, he seemed comfortable and quite at home in the unpretentious surroundings. Her heart skipped a beat as she surveyed his handsome face, dark hair with a persistent errant lock that dangled over his forehead. It gave Patrick Ryan an impish look, yet with his six-foot plus you could hardly say "imp".

She leaned slightly toward Ryan. "I've had the occasion of meeting several people in town. A few at the courthouse and Mr. Brown, my parents' lawyer." She straightened and flipped an errant lock of her dark hair over her shoulder.

"Yes, I know BB. He does fairly well since he is the only lawyer in town."

Her eyebrows raised. She remembered Sue Bader telling her the same thing. "I don't imagine there is much legal work to be done in Moultrie."

Ryan turned and looked directly at Laura. "I'm sure business will grow with the anticipation of the new highway and building growth."

She studied the seriousness of his gray-blue eyes. "Well, that would mean just condemnation suits of land acquisition. Cut and dried. Nothing covering the spectrum of legal expertise."

"I think, with the highway and new ground broken, so to speak, there would be an influx of new families and housing. The demand for legal assistance would come."

"You're talking years down the road."

"No, not really. Surveyors are working, already, and it will just be a matter of a short time when the state will approach for legal work."

Laura frowned in thought. "I see."

The butler appeared in the doorway, announced, "Dinner is served," and returned to the kitchen.

Laura was delighted at the array of food. The buffet held a sizzling hot platter of thick slices of prime rib, a serving dish of twice baked potatoes, and a chafing dish with carrot casserole. The water glasses were filled, and the opened wine had been set next to a setting. She assumed it was where Robert had placed his employer.

"Shall I serve, Mr. Pat?"

"No, Robert, we will serve ourselves."

With a nod the butler returned to the kitchen.

"I see you can really prepare a proper dinner under extraordinary circumstances".

"Not I, but Mrs. Taylor, my cook."

Noticing the extra serving pieces of silverware and china Laura remarked, "Robert seems to have found his way around the kitchen"

"That's because he has been in your kitchen many times."

"Really! How did that happen?"

"He has helped your mother on several occasions when she entertained. I'm sure he knows where everything is in the kitchen."

They settled down to enjoy their dinner, mixed with light conversation. Patrick Ryan discussed his last trip to New York to hear his son, Kevin's, piano concert to which Laura was both surprised and impressed.

"The Julliard School of Music, that's quite an accomplishment to be accepted there."

"Yes, and he is quite accomplished."

"I didn't know you had a son. How old is he?"

"He'll be seventeen this year. I've been divorced six years now."

Laura changed the subject and spoke of her role in the Richmond law firm of Katz, Katz and Katz.

"I notice there isn't any enthusiasm in your voice as you tell me about your role."

"No, I am just another lawyer in a firm of approximately 50. I guess you can say I'm just another cog in the wheel."

They continued their conversation and enjoyed the Bordeaux. Robert appeared and asked if all was well.

"Yes, Robert, and did Mrs. Taylor send anything to finish off the dinner?"

"Indeed! Indeed! Somethin' special, Mr. Pat. I'll bring it in ri now" With a huge tray he removed the china and silverware and went back into the kitchen. In a few minutes he returned with compote glasses, her mother's, filled with fresh strawberries and cream, dripping with chocolate coating.

Laura's jaw would have gaped if she didn't have herself under control.

Ryan saw the sparkle in her eyes. "I'm glad the dessert pleases you."

"The entire dinner was exceptional, for which I thank you."

Finishing dessert, they returned to the living room where Laura saw a bottle of liquor, with appropriate glasses, had been set on a tray.

"Frangelico. My favorite, How did you know?"

"It's what you ordered at the club the other night."

"So you were our anonymous host."

"Yes, I happened to be there when you came in with Caper Morgan."

"She was kind enough to invite me to dinner. I didn't realize she was a friend to my mother."

Patrick Ryan opened the bottle and poured the golden syrupy liquid. "Judith and Caper were fairly close." He handed a glass to Laura. "Here's to your decision," and he touched his glass to hers.

Laura took a sip, relaxed back into the cushions and turned toward Ryan. "Okay, Mr. Ryan, suppose you tell me just why you are wining and dining me. What's the catch?"

"No 'catch'. I just want to reiterate my desire to purchase your property if you put it up for sale."

"I haven't decided as yet."

"Understandable. It's a big decision."

Robert came to the doorway. "Mr. Pat. I've cleaned up", and turning to Laura, he said, "and Miz Crowder I put all the serving pieces away. Leftovers are in the 'frigerator. I'll be leaving now."

"Thank you, Robert," Laura gave him an appreciative smile, "and please tell Mrs. Taylor that the dinner was one of the finest I've eaten."

"Thank you, Miz Crowder, "I'll be sure to tell her. She will be very pleased." The butler left and soon the motor of the SUV could be heard droning away.

Laura turned to Patrick Ryan. "Now tell me Mr. Ryan, just why is it so all-fired important for you to buy this place?"

"I'd like to combine the two properties. The piece I have contains only fifteen acres. Since your property is also fifteen acres it would give me a nice parcel of land."

"Do you plan to subdivide?"

"God forbid!" He moved closer to Laura. "It would give me a little more room. Like you, I like my own space."

Unaware she was frowning, Ryan said, "What seems to be the problem?"

"Ambivalence." She sipped her liquor. "I know I have to do something but I'm not sure what I want to do."

Ryan finished his drink and reached for Laura's hand. "I think I'll let you sleep on it. Sooner or later you will come to a decision." He got to his feet and Laura did the same.

"Again I want to thank you for the dinner. It truly was delicious."

Together they walked to the front door and without further ado Patrick swept Laura into his arms and planted a full kiss upon her lips.

"The first kiss I gave you was to seal a bargain. This one is for a lovely evening well spent." Then he was gone.

Laura still felt the tingle of his kiss as she climbed the stairs to her bedroom muttering, "I got to watch out for that guy."

* * * * *

At the time Laura and Patrick were enjoying dinner, Cheryl Tanner, a beautician, was tucking her six month old son, Tommy, into his crib. When she returned to the kitchen she turned up the volume of the baby intercom so she could hear Tommy if he got restless. The baby intercom had a quirk of picking up neighborhood phone conversations when certain weather conditions prevailed. Beside the baby intercom was a police scanner that picked up the police frequency and other weird calls. Fred, her husband, worked for the South Carolina Department of Transportation (SCDOT) as a mechanic at their district garage in Moultrie County, but was also on call as a volunteer fireman, and used the police scanner to alert him to any reported house fires. It, too, picked up unwanted messages at times. Between the two scanners, the system was a veritable communications center, albeit sometimes a bit embarrassing. Needless to say, Cheryl had bits of news and information to pique her customers' interests.

As she was washing the dinner dishes a garbled voice came on the scanner asking for assistance from AAA. She remembered a similar message on the night Amelia Talbot called AAA then disappeared. A cold chill swept over her and she shook with the feeling. She wondered if the Milford Garage or the police department would follow-up. The police scanner was quiet. It was Friday night and most likely the small police department was on less than half-staff. But someone had to be manning the phones in both places.

Cheryl finished the dishes and after checking in on Tommy she went into the living room to watch TV and wait up for Fred. He was at the fire station attending a method and instruction meeting. He was a very conscientious fireman.

* * * * *

Sandra Perkins ended her mobile phone call to AAA. As instructed, she waited for the Milford Garage wrecker. She chastised herself for not watching the gas gauge.

"Stupid of me to run out of gas," she muttered and clicked the button to lock all the car doors.

When the engine started to sputter, she was smart enough to pull the car to the side of the road. She didn't want to be caught in the middle of the highway. She leaned forward and turned on the interior lights. It had only been a few minutes since she phoned AAA. She took the prepared booklet from the banking meeting and scanned the first sheet. A slash of headlights came from behind her car obliterating any recognition. Sandra Perkins held her breath until a familiar voice told her to roll down her car window.

"Miz Perkins, I came out to take you into town. It's too dangerous to be out here alone."

"Oh, thank you so much. I was a bit worried."

"Not to worry. Put the key on top of the visor, take your purse and unlock the doors so they can pull your car up onto the wrecker bed."

Sandra grabbed her purse, the strap to her phone bag, the prepared booklet from the banking meeting, and climbed out of the car. She followed her rescuer to his truck and with his help mounted the passenger side seat.

"I'm so glad you picked me up, I was concerned about being here all alone."

"I'm sure you were. My, but you smell wonderful. Nice perfume."

Sandra smiled. "Thank you."

As they drove off, Sandra busied herself with putting the banking booklet into her purse and paid no attention as to where she was being driven. When it dawned on her that it was not in the general direction of town she said, "Where are we going?"

With a strong right hand, the driver knocked her unconscious. When she came to she was in a wooded area, on the ground, and knew her clothes had been opened or torn off the front of her body. Her slacks had been removed as well as her panties.

"What the hell are you doing?" She struggled to get to her feet.

He punched her back down. "You just stay there. You aint goin' nowhere."

He grabbed for her breast and squeezed it. "All the time you sittin' back behind that bank glass, saying, 'Can I help you?' well now you can." As he spoke he worked at the fly of his hunting pants. Camouflaged pattern. He pulled out his fully erected penis and dropped down on top of Sandra, poking with his sex organ, seeking her entry.

Sandra tried to turn her body away from the assault. "Get the hell off me you bastard."

He raised his hand and slapped her across the face. "Don't call me a bastard, I had a mama and daddy." He thrust his strong hand down on her throat. "You're gonna do as I tell ya."

58

His erection pushed into Sandra and she let out a gasp of pain. She knew she was losing the battle. He pumped into her with brutal force and she relaxed to ease the pain.

Thinking about her survival, she said, "Why didn't you tell me you wanted to fuck me."

He stopped dead. "You mean you like it?"

"Well, if you had given me a little time I could have warmed up to the occasion."

"Well, that's more like it." He proceeded with easy strokes and moved his calloused hand over her breast. His fingers found the nipple and he pinched it roughly.

Sandra's mind was spinning, trying to think of ways to come out of this alive. She knew he would kill her. She pushed up against him.

"That's it, baby. Give it to me."

She stretched out her arms hoping to find a stone or something to use to hit him but there was nothing. She slid her hands down the side of his body as he rhythmically engaged in his lust. Her hand touched the haft of the hunting knife in its sheath and she gently pulled it out.

His voice bellowed as he reached his sexual climax. Sandra slashed the knife across his face and he screamed and fell off her. Once more she tried to get to her feet but he pulled her down, rolled on top of her body and took the knife from her hand. With the ease of gutting a rabbit, he slashed her throat then went to the truck for the tarpaulin.

CHAPTER 6

April is a beautiful month in South Carolina. This realization struck Laura as she drove out the driveway and headed toward the town of Moultrie. She slowed as she passed the entry to ERIN. Craning her neck, she tried to see the residence but could not. Miffed, she increased her speed, passed the Hilltop Motel and entered town.

Saturday appeared to be a busy day for Moultrie. Tourists milled about the square seemingly not in a hurry to do anything. Laura parked her car facing the Confederate Monument, got out and walked to George's Sandwich Shop. Sue Bader came out of the eatery and met her.

"I'm so glad you could make it. Ya sounded a bit *iffy* when I called."

"I was. Should we use my car?"

"No, I'm parked on the side street. I know what I'd like to show you and where it is, so all you have to do is gawk at the sights." Sue led the way to her small car.

Laura smiled at the young woman. "I'm sure I'll be doing a lot of 'gawking'. Can't imagine what there is to be seen."

"Well, like I said, I can have you back here by four."

Laura nodded and got into the passenger side.

Sue Bader drove slowly towards the outskirts of town, slowing up as they passed a large brick mill.

"In the '30s, this mill produced a crucial bit of evidence in a murder trial. Seems the twine made here was the same as the twine that bound the hands and feet of a murder victim. The mill manager had to appear and give evidence that the twine was made in his plant. The crime lab had a way of identifying and matching the fibers. If you're wondering where I got the info, I read the county history when I first came down from Cleveland."

"It's a wonder you aren't working for the Chamber of Commerce."

"No, I'm very satisfied working for the County Planning Commission." She jabbed her finger at the median strip. "Your dad planned and supervised the planting of the strip. He really did a beautiful job."

Laura saw the pink and white azaleas shrubs that stretched down the median as a backdrop for the flowering iris and dusty miller. A lump formed in Laura's throat. "It's very beautiful."

"Now, if you drive further east on 57 you'll pass Edward's Lunch Shack. Edward is George's brother and between them they have the lunch crowd sewed up. Edward serves hamburgers, hot dogs, hoagies and subs. Strictly for the blue-collar crowd including the illegals. No waitresses. Wraps every order in butcher paper. You pay for it and find a place to eat. He has picnic tables outside for use in nice weather. Even the Moultrie emergency crew and police eat there. I was told that someone said Edward served the same way as did COTTON'S down in Corpus Christi, Texas. I've never been to Texas so I can't say if that's true."

Sue turned off Highway 57 onto a county road. After passing several fields she pointed to a long low-level wooden home with a wrap-around porch. "That's where Joellyn and Charles Godwin live." She swept her hand across the horizon. "He owns all of that land. I took Joellyn's job when she married him."

"He must be very prosperous."

"Is."

About five miles out of Moultrie Sue pointed to the stone pillars with the name plaque MOULTRIE COMMONS.

"This is the new independent living community which includes assisted living and an Alzheimer facility. It's just getting off the ground, so to speak. Opened a year ago. It's pulling a lot of people from the big city."

Laura caught glimpses of a huge stone structure several stories high, with an elegant entrance. Single story stone wings reached out on both sides of the main building. It reminded her of an English estate.

"Now, I'll show you the lake and dam."

Laura sat up straight as they approached the lake. She could see the dam intake turrets and the highway that crossed. The lake itself was impressively large. When Sue turned east on the road along the lake, she pointed to the sign LAKESIDE.

"That's where Millie's parents live. I stop by and see them every once in awhile."

She drove across the dam and Laura got a full view of the length of the lake. It looked several miles long.

"What a beautiful sight."

"You should see it when they hold a regatta. Sails everywhere."

"Didn't realize there were so many sailing enthusiasts."

"Oh yeah. Even your neighbor, Patrick Ryan, gets involved. He uses a small sail boat for the regatta which he keeps berthed somewhere on the lake. He has a really big one, the *Killarney,* down at Harbour Town Yacht Basin on Hilton Head Island. I've been on that one."

"How did you manage that?"

"Through Millie. As I said, one of these days I'll tell you all about Millie and me and the killer, Gerald Brown, but right now I'm going to turn around and re-cross the dam, swing west and show you the Moultrie Correctional Unit."

Sue drove several miles up the county road until they were passing the correctional unit. Two stories high, barred windows, and a chain-link fence topped with barbed wire.

"There it is. Not too bad considering it's a jail. Got a large athletic field behind. The guys in there aren't dangerous. They just made stupid mistakes. Most of them are drop-outs with little education. Weather permitting, the warden gets them out for road work. Some have gardens in the back field."

"Do any of them try to escape?"

Why would they do that? Their homes are in Moultrie. They ain't going any place but Moultrie. Their momas and daddies are waiting for them to get out. I know a few that when they got out they went back to school for their diplomas and then got jobs right in Moultrie."

"Sounds like a good rehabilitation plan."

"You betcha!"

A few miles past the jail Sue turned her car eastward onto Highway 57.

"We're heading back toward Moultrie now. We'll be passing your place and ERIN, Ryan's place."

"Good. Why not stop by my place and I'll show you around?"

"Sounds good to me."

Laura watched closely as they drove along so that she would not miss the entrance to the driveway. Seeing it, she indicated to Sue the turn and the car turned onto the driveway.

"Holy Shlamoly. That's quite a place." Sue parked the car, got out and stood staring up at the facade.

"Yes, it is," Laura said as she got out of the car. "My mom always wanted a stone house, like they build in Pennsylvania."

"It's beautiful. I can see your dad's garden work all around the place."

"Yes, I can, too." Laura unlocked the front door and beckoned Sue to enter. "I think I have some ice tea in the fridge. Want some?"

"Sounds good to me." Sue followed Laura into the kitchen, craning her neck to see the rooms they passed through and to take in the modern kitchen design. "Wow, what a place."

"It is beautiful, isn't it."

"And you're thinking of selling this place? Boy, if I could afford it, I'd snatch it up in a New York minute."

Laura was glad she got the chair cushions from the garage storage that morning. They appeared almost new. "Let's sit out on the patio."

Sue and Laura settled themselves into the comfortable padded aluminum chairs.

"What a beautiful view," Sue murmured. "I can see why your dad was so crazy about this place. He was always talking about it."

"I'm glad they were happy here," Laura whispered.

"They sure were." Sue reached over and pat Laura's hand. "I don't think wild horses could have pulled them away."

They sipped their tea in silence and then Sue said, "I guess I'd better get you back to town so you can pick up your car. Glad you decided to go so I could show you a small part of Moultrie."

"It was very interesting." Laura got up and Sue followed her into the kitchen. They set their glasses in the sink, and headed toward the front door.

Back in Sue's small car Laura felt at ease for the first time since she arrived in Moultrie. She glanced at Sue's profile. *Cute gal. Crackling blue eyes. Ivory complexion. Nice figure and long blonde hair.* "Sue, if I'm not being too personal, are you married or going with anyone?"

"Not married. Hope to be. I'm going with one of the guys in the office. It's Saturday and we have a date for tonight."

"That doesn't interfere with your work relationship?"

"No. I work directly for Mr. Pierce, the commissioner. Pete's one of the commission's agents." She hurriedly pointed to the gates of ERIN. "That's Ryan's place. Right next door to yours."

"Yes, I know. One of these days I'll pay Mr. Ryan a visit. He doesn't seem to mind coming over and visiting with me."

"Oh, really! Yes, that's right, you told me he made an offer to buy your place." Sue turned toward Laura. "Don't sell just yet. Give yourself some time."

They drove passed Hilltop Motel and into Moultrie. Sue parked in the same place as she did earlier and they got out.

"I hope you liked our little jaunt. I'll show you the rest of Moultrie another day."

Laura was going to shake Sue's hand but changed her mind and hugged her. "Thanks so much, Sue. I did enjoy our 'jaunt'."

Sue got into her car and with a wave, drove off.

Laura went out to the square, got into her car and headed back to her place. Half-way home something snapped in her mind.

Sue said she was dating one of the guys in the office. That Pete was one of the commission's agents. Dad's letter said his son, Peter Harris, worked for the County Planning Commission. My God! Sue must be dating my half-brother.

* * * * *

While fixing a light supper, Laura turned on the radio to the local news. The news announcer was reporting on the disappearance of yet another local citizen. "Sandra Perkins, a teller at the Moultrie Bank was reported missing by her parents this morning. Yesterday she attended a banking conference in Columbia and her colleagues stated she left for home at about seven Friday evening."

"My God," Laura said aloud. "I just met her the other day at the bank. A lovely young girl. What the hell is going on in this town?" She visually recalled the young teller whose name tag said Sandra Perkins. "This seems more than coincidence. Do we have a serial killer here in Moultrie?" A chill swept down her spine and she shivered with the feeling.

I've got one more week here, she thought, I just can't handle all that I have to do in that short of time. I'm going to have to call Katz, et al, and ask them to extend my leave. I'll call Monday.

With a piece of last night's leftover cold roast beef wrapped in a lettuce leaf, she carried her plate into her father's den, sat at the desk and munched, all the time thinking of what she had to do. She had to contact a legal

65

mediator to handle the transfer of stocks, bonds and insurance left to Peter Harris, and to keep herself out of the picture. It was important to her father that Peter Harris not learn of his birth father. She guessed it would have to be a lawyer in Columbia and that would take a bit of research. But who? There was only one person she could name that would have the scope of knowledge to help her. Patrick Ryan.

Damn, I hate to call on him for advice but it would save a lot of time trying to check MARTINDALE-HUBBELL, and that would be just a shot in the dark.

She found his name in the local directory and punched in the numbers.

"The Ryan residence."

"This is Laura Crowder."

"Oh, yes, Miz Crowder. What can I do for you?"

"Is Mr. Ryan at home?"

"Yes, Miz, I'll fetch him."

It was a matter of seconds when Patrick Ryan picked up the receiver. "Yes, Laura, what is it?"

His voice held an urgency, as if worried.

"I hate to bother you at this time of night, but I want to ask, if you were in need of a lawyer, a mediator so to speak, who would you hire?"

His light chuckled rankled her. "I don't mean to amuse, Mr. Ryan, but I am in need of a discretionary legal beagle, as the saying goes. Not all lawyers are discreet and I was hoping you could save me a lot of time, and possibly some embarrassment."

He must have noticed her serious tenor for he quickly said, "Not knowing the nature of your business, but knowing a very good all around lawyer in Columbia, I would recommend Carleton Dinford. He handled some matters for me on the side that I did not wish to become public."

Laura's thoughts shot through what Ryan said. She wondered if it could be a payoff for a breech of promise or an illegitimate child. He seemed to fit the bill for a philanderer.

"Could you give me his telephone number?" She wrote it down and made a mental note to call on Monday. It seemed Monday was going to be a busy day.

*****

She awoke early. It was Sunday morning. Her parents had always attended church when they lived in Richmond and Laura was sure they had continued the practice here in Moultrie. She showered, dressed in her business suit, and drove into Moultrie.

On the four corners of the block above the town square sat four churches. Laura smiled. *They cover all the denominations.* She found the one of her parents' faith, parked her car and entered the church. Service would begin at ten o'clock. The church was already full. She felt edgy since it had been some time since she had been to church. She slipped into the back pew, acknowledged with a smile the friendly nods, and sat. A few minutes before ten o'clock the usher asked her to slip down as another was being seated. She did so with her eyes forward.

The long trousered legs looked familiar and she glanced up into the smiling face of Patrick Ryan. She could feel the flush spread over her face as he nodded to her.

"Good morning," he softly said.

Laura nodded and focused her eyes on the altar.

How could I have chosen the same church as Patrick Ryan? Him, a reprobate, a philanderer, definitely a lady's man. I can't imagine him as being a church goer.

"All rise and greet Reverend Nicholson."

The minister appeared to be in his mid-sixties. A thick shock of gray hair topped a well chiseled face. His erect, almost military stance displayed a trim, athletic body.

Laura was surprised when the minister mentioned the disappearance of two of his parishioners, Amelia Talbot and Sandra Perkins, and asked that they be remembered in our prayers.

Throughout the service Laura was extremely cognizant of her inner feelings, the closeness of the man, especially when she and Patrick shared the Hymnal. She wanted to leave but would have had to pass in front of him. Her behind just inches from his face. No, she could not leave and steadied her nerves until the end of the service.

Reverend Nicholson stood at the front portal and was shaking everyone's hand. He was especially exuberant when he came to Ryan.

"How are you, Patrick?" Not waiting for an answer he continued, "We thank you so much for," he glanced at Laura and said, "attending. Now, who is this young lady?" His spectacled eyes peered into Laura's.

Laura felt as if under a microscope as Ryan said, "May I introduce Miss Laura Crowder, Philip and Judith's daughter from Richmond, Virginia."

"Welcome, my dear," and he grasped Laura's hand and firmly shook it then softly added, "and please accept my condolences on their demise. Unfortunate, very unfortunate."

Laura managed to thank the cleric and moved passed Ryan and headed for her car.

Ryan caught up with her and placed his hand on her elbow. "Don't hurry off. I'd like to talk to you. I was a bit surprised when I saw you in church, but then again, I don't know why. Judith and Philip attended every Sunday.

Laura turned and faced Ryan. "You saw them in church every Sunday?" She realized how stupid that sounded. "I mean, I know my parents would regularly attend service, I just didn't realize you did."

"Do you think me some sinner?"

Again Laura's face flushed. "I didn't mean that as it sounded." She flustered with her purse and gloves.

"You're forgiven."

Her fingers found the car remote and was about to unlock the vehicle when Ryan laid his hand over hers. "I was planning on going into Greenwood for brunch. Would you care to join me?" He saw the negative look composing on her face and quickly added, "Then I can tell you about my conversation with Carleton Dinford regarding your up-coming visit."

Laura released the huff of her intended reply and frowned. "You called him?"

"Yes. He happens to be a friend of mine. Now, why don't you join me for brunch and I can tell you all about him."

"I guess I could", she grudging conceded. "I have no other plans."

"It's a place called *Inn on the Square*. They have a very nice buffet.

* * * * *

Ryan drove down what was purported to be the widest street in the country. A median strip separated the through traffic, and side access streets fronted the businesses. Laura noted that most of the businesses were lawyers.

"They must do a lot of legal work in this town judging from the number of legal shingles. Why do you go to Columbia when there are so many lawyers here to choose from?"

"I know a few lawyers here, but I prefer to keep my business farther afield. Besides, not many local lawyers are proficient in international law."

"Oh, yes, I forgot. Your business moves in international circles."

"Exactly."

"And what exactly is your business?"

"I told you I was in the diamond business, and a few other enterprises."

She was about to ask more when Ryan pulled into a parking area next to what appeared as a three storey boxy-looking building.

"Here we are."

Laura was pleasantly surprised by the comfortable interior of the lobby and lounge. Patrick took her arm and guided her down a short hall into the dining room.

A long buffet was set in the middle of the room displaying various dishes of enticing food. A cauldron of soup dominated one end of the table. As they walked past mouth-savoring aromas rose from the selection of foods, and she could smell the garlic rub on the roast tenderloin. Various other meats and a variety of vegetables and salads filled the table. A side buffet held an assortment of desserts fluffed with dollops of whipped cream. Laura felt her stomach jump with joy.

Patrick held her chair as she sat. "I have to apologize," he murmured, "it's Sunday, and South Carolina has Blue Laws. They don't serve alcohol on Sunday so I can't order wine. I guess I should have taken you to the club."

"No, this is fine. It's something new to me. It's very relaxed." She looked about and noted young families. "I think this is quite nice."

"Good! Let's pick up some salad or fruit to start."

Ryan led the way to the buffet and they both enjoyed selecting their small salad. As they sat, Laura gave a deep sigh.

"That sounds sad. What's the trouble?"

"Nothing," Laura responded, "just that I thought the minister was so considerate in mentioning the two missing women."

"It's serious business when two women disappear from Moultrie and in such a short time and no one has heard from them since"

"I've been thinking, Mr. Ryan, do you think we have a serial killer in our midst?"

"First, please call me Patrick, and if I may I will call you Laura. Now, with that taken care of, no, I don't think we have a serial killer in Moultrie."

Laura frowned. "You know, speaking of serial killers, in a few days they will be executing Timothy Spence in

Richmond. He murdered four women and was convicted on DNA samples. Are you familiar with DNA?"

"I've read about it. Something about matching the thread of life. It's supposed to be with a high degree of accuracy."

"Yes, a one to ten billion ratio of accuracy. It's been mentioned in the AMA and the ABA mags since '86 and bears a strong impact on legal proceedings. My field."

"Talking about killings, BB, you know, Butler Brown called me last night on some business and mentioned that one of our police officers had killed an illegal outside of Edward's Lunch Shack last night. Seems, according to BB, the illegal was drunk and pulled a knife. The officer shot him. There will be a hearing on it. BB will handle it." Patrick put his hand over Laura's. "Well, let's forget business and killings for now. Bon appétit."

Patrick Ryan and Laura enjoyed going up to the buffet and selecting entrées and vegetables, each making comments about their choices. Sometimes with laughter.

"I promised to tell you about Carleton Dinford. I met him through some business acquaintances and probed into his clients relationships. Asked a lot of questions and came up with nothing. I decided he had integrity and I ask him if he would take me on as a client, with an annual retainer. Dinford accepted so I handed him a "hot potato". I wanted to buy the building on Main street in town but I didn't want anyone to know who was buying until the sale was completed. He did an excellent job, kept my name out of it, and even after the sale he would not divulge the name of the buyer. I did, myself, when I went to record the deed. I am very pleased with Carleton Dinford and how he conducts business. I highly recommend him to you."

"Thank you, Patrick, I feel a lot better. I'll call him tomorrow morning."

Ryan drove Laura back to the church. She felt a feeling of well-being as she thanked him for a pleasant luncheon and bid him good day,

When she got home, she kicked off her shoes, plopped down on the sofa and, with a silly smile on her face, rested her head on a pillow and fell asleep.

CHAPTER 7

Monday was a test. First, she had to call Katz et al and ask for an extension of time to which they agreed but without pay. Then Carleton Dinford in Columbia to make an appointment which he set for 9:30 Wednesday morning of this week. That suited Laura and she had the feeling Patrick Ryan's influence had something to do with the earliness of the appointment. Dinford was squeezing her into his set docket. He never asked the nature of her visit. That, too, she credited to Ryan.

After breakfast, she drove into Moultrie, parked behind the courthouse, and decided to visit Caper Morgan. The old-time cowbells jingled as she entered. The saleswoman, recognizing Laura from her first visit, waved her back to Caper's office. Laura knocked, was bid enter, and she walked in and dropped into the chair across from Caper Morgan.

"You look a little testy," Caper said.

"I guess you can say that. I'm up to my neck in problems."

"Well, you can lean on Caper's shoulder, if you want."

Laura studied the woman's classic profile, her beautifully coiffed blonde-gray hair pulled up into a French twist, and her elegant attire. "I really need advice, and it is of a very personal matter, Caper. Do you think you want to hear?"

"Hell, yes. Your mom used to come in and we'd let our hair down. She was one great gal and I miss her terribly."

"Mom came in to discuss personal matters with you?"

"Yes, and wild horses couldn't drag them out of me."

Laura stared into the woman's blue eyes and neither turned their gaze. It was almost like reading each other's mind.

"You know?"

"Have known ever since Judith confided in me."

"You mean about the *set aside* stocks, bonds and insurance?"

"Exactly! And I know who is the recipient of those funds. When I called you and asked you to go to the club with me I knew that you had found the letter."

Laura pulled back in astonishment. "How did you know?"

"You forget, I told you Judith and I were close, very close."

"But how could she tell you the contents of the letter? It was sealed."

"We did a good job of resealing it after Judith read it."

"Mom knew? Oh, my God."

"Your mother loved your father, in her heart she forgave him his indiscretion. Actually, she befriended Pete Harris. She thought him a fine young man."

Tears rolled down Laura's cheeks. "Poor Mom, she must have been hurt terribly."

"No. She was at first, then I remember she re-read your father's letter and smiled. She knew there was something in Moultrie that drew him here. The place is nowhere. It really was the answer to a puzzle."

"I guess that's why Dad volunteered with the County Beautification Commission, to see his son once in a while."

"Exactly! Now, not to be too nosey, how do you plan to handle the distribution of those *set aside* investments?"

"I have an appointment with Carleton Dinford in Columbia who, I trust, will make the proper arrangements and keep my name out of it."

"Oh, that he'll do. Carleton is very discreet."

"You know him?"

"Over the years he has become a friend of mine."

"Maybe I should have called you instead of Patrick Ryan."

"You called Ryan?"

"Yes, and he talked to Dinford to arrange an early appointment."

"Yes, Ryan could do that. I think he pays Dinford an annual retainer."

"Well, I have an appointment with Dinford on Wednesday. I'll take all the necessary papers, including dad's letter, and see what he advises." Laura stood.

Caper got up, came around her desk and hugged Laura.

"Whenever you feel like a little company or want to let your hair down, call me."

Laura kissed Caper on the cheek. "It's good to have a friend." She sniffled, and left the office.

Outside, the town of Moultrie was busy with tourists. She glanced at her watch and saw it was a quarter after eleven. Crossing the brick paved street, she entered the County Administration Building. She remembered Sue Bader telling her the Moultrie Planning Commission was on the second floor. Reluctantly, she climbed the stairs, strode to the back of the hall and entered the office.

A man, dressed for no respect, looked up, saw Laura and quickly stood. His face mirrored his licentious thoughts.

"Can I help you?" He held out his hand. "My name is Carey Thomas but everyone calls me CT."

Laura accepted his hand. "Laura Crowder. I'm looking for Sue Bader."

"She's in with the ol' man right now. She'll be out in a few minutes. Wont you sit down?" He indicated a wooden armchair.

"Thank you, but I don't want to take up any more of your time."

"You can take all the time you want," he smirked.

"May I leave a message?"

"Of course."

Laura saw no note paper was being offered. "Please tell her Laura Crowder would like to have lunch with her. I'll wait down stairs."

"I'll do that. I assume you'll have lunch at George's?"

Laura gave the man a steely stare, "Not necessarily", and spun on her heels and left.

Downstairs, she settled on the hall bench and waited for Sue. It wasn't long before the vivacious blonde bounced down the stairs and rushed to Laura.

"Gee, I'm glad to see you. I think it's a great idea to have lunch together. If you don't want to go to George's there's Edward's Lunch Shack like I told you Saturday, but I got to tell you, Laura, It's not for you. Besides, there was a killing there on Saturday night."

Laura held up her hand to stop Sue's verbal flow. "I was thinking of taking you to the country club. Would you care to go?"

Sue's eyes widened. "Sure would. Haven't been there. A little out of my range."

Sue followed Laura to her Mercedes and they were soon at the club. The cool, somber interior was brightened by a huge floral arrangement on the over-sized mahogany table in the reception room. Sue touched the soft petals of the calla lilies and stretched to sniff their fragrance, surprised to find very little. She shrugged, as if to say the beauty of the lilies was enough.

Laura took Sue by the arm and led her to Edmond's station.

"Good afternoon, Miss Crowder. Very nice to see you again," purred the maitre d'.

"Thank you, Edmond," and turning toward Sue she said, "and this is Miss Sue Bader, my guest."

"Very nice to have you here, Miss Bader."

Sue nodded and mumbled, "Thank you."

The maitre d' turned to Laura. "Do you have any particular seating in mind, Miss Crowder?"

"A table by the rear windows, please Edmond."

"Right this way, please."

The table for two overlooked the tenth fairway and a broad expanse of the lake. Sue's eyes swept the interior of the dining room and the magnificent view and softly hissed between her teeth.

"Lord, this is some place."

"Glad you approve."

Edmond held Laura's chair as she was seated then quickly moved to hold Sue's. He proved to be the epitome of efficiency. He took the folded napkin, snapped it open and placed it on Laura's lap, then handed her the menu.

Sue quickly took her napkin and placed it on her lap much to Edmond's chagrin.

He handed Sue the menu, turned to Laura and said, "I will send Shirley over to take your order, Miss Crowder."

"Thank you, Edmond."

"Wow! This is some place," Sue whispered across the table.

"It's just a restaurant, albeit an elegant one."

"You can say that again."

"I recommend the grilled chicken salad. It's fresh, tasty and quick knowing you have limited time."

"Sounds good to me."

Laura gave the waitress the orders and settled back into the chair. "I want to thank you for taking me for our 'jaunt' on Saturday. I really did enjoy it."

"And I want to thank you for taking me to your home for iced tea. You have a beautiful home, Laura."

"Yes, it is a beautiful place. It's beginning to grow on me. I feel so comfortable and secure there."

"Well, that tells you something, doesn't it? Just don't be in too much of a rush to sell."

"I'm thinking about it." Laura pushed her utensils aside and leaned toward the perky blonde. "Sue, what do you know about the new highway that's supposed to come through the county?"

"Only what Pete tells me. It's on the drawing board and engineers are working with the local highway agents so I'm sure it's a go. In fact, several people have been contacted with land purchase offers. The highway is supposed to be built east of Moultrie, cutting across Route 57."

Laura vaguely heard what Sue said. Her thoughts were on Pete. The mention of his name brought back thoughts of her mother and Caper knowing about her father's illegitimate son; her half-brother.

"Speaking of Pete," Laura said softly, "have you made any definite wedding plans?"

"Lord, no," Sue said, dropping her eyes, "he hasn't asked me yet."

"Do you like him?"

"Like him, I'm crazy about him. He's the sweetest guy."

"Well, that sounds promising. I hope he pops the question."

"He's so practical, and says he's saving up before he takes the big step. I just can't push the guy."

Laura thought of the windfall coming to Peter Harris from her father's estate. She reached over and pat Sue's hand. "Don't worry. It may come sooner than you think."

The waitress, Shirley, placed the cold salad plates and iced tea before them, and turned to Laura. "Will there be anything else?"

"No, thank you, Shirley." Laura nodded to Sue, "Enjoy!"

During the luncheon Sue said, "You've got to meet Pete. He's wonderful."

"I'm sure I will some day," Laura responded. She glanced at her watch. "Got to get you back to the office. Don't want to cause any trouble between you and your boss."

"Nah! Mr. Pierce is a pussy cat. A real nice guy to work for."

They finished their lunch, got into Laura's Mercedes and drove back into Moultrie. Sue repeated her many thanks and Laura drove back to her home.

* * * * *

Early Wednesday morning, Laura drove down to Columbia to keep her appointment with Carleton Dinford. With Map-Quest in hand, she had a vague idea where to find the law office located somewhere around the many cross-sections of Main Street.

The building was multi-storied. Taking the elevator to the third floor, she stepped out into the vestibule where an efficient-looking receptionist greeted her.

"Miss Crowder?"

"Yes, I'm Laura Crowder."

"Mr. Dinford is expecting you." She got up from behind the desk and led Laura into an inner reception room elegantly furnished. "He'll be with you in a moment."

Laura observed the posh decor, the dark wood paneling and ornate ceiling molding and figured Carleton Dinford had a very lucrative practice.

The double doors opened and a smartly dressed man, about sixty, moved with authority toward her, hand extended. "Miss Crowder, how nice to meet you." He took Laura's extended hand. "Please come into my office."

Office was hardly the word. The room took in the whole corner of the building facing two streets. Glass from ceiling to floor. An oversized desk squatted at an angle across the corner of the room and the lawyer agilely slipped behind it. With a wave of his arm he indicated for Laura to sit.

"Mr. Ryan informed me of the loss of your parents. Please accept my condolences. Now, how can I be of assistance?"

"I thank you for seeing me on such short notice. It's very kind of you."

She settled into an upholstered armchair facing Dinford and placed on her lap the leather folder of stocks, bonds, policies and the proper number of death certificates. Looking straight into his eyes, she said, "I have been told that you are discreet and can be trusted with information that is better left private."

Dinford smiled. "Yes, I can be trusted."

She handed her father's letter to the lawyer. He read it and glanced up. "I can assume you had no idea of the existence of your half-brother?"

"None."

"And you wish to carry out your father's wishes?"

"I do."

"Of course, as executrix, you can either honor, or not, the commission."

"I shall honor it. It was my father's wish. Can this be done discreetly and my name remain anonymous?"

"Yes, I can make all the stock transfers and insurance payments as your representative, if that is agreeable with you."

"Yes, it is."

The lawyer pressed the intercom button and spoke. "Mrs. Seigler, please come in."

A door to the left opened and a tall, well tailored woman entered, steno pad in hand. "Yes, Mr. Dinford?"

Laura assumed the receptionist was the secretary, but this was another person. A legal assistant.

"This is Miss Laura Crowder from Moultrie. I will be representing her in some very personal matters. Please bring me a contract for her to sign."

The woman spun around and was back in a moment, contract in hand. She handed it to Dinford, her eyebrows rose as if to ask the question.

"That will be all Mrs. Seigler."

He handed the contract to Laura and she quickly perused it, seeing it was much the same as that used in the Katz firm. She took the offered pen, signed her name, then handed the folder of papers over to Dinford.

"I believe you will find all the necessary papers in there. How long do you think it will take to activate the changes and make payment of the insurance?"

"I shall write them today. Did you include the death certificates?"

"Yes, there all in there."

"Your telephone number?"

Laura gave him her parents' phone number and handed him her business card. "This is in case I have to return to Richmond."

Dinford glanced at the card. "And how is Isador Katz,

tough ol' codger."

"You know Mr. Katz, senior?"

"Met him at a bar association conference in Richmond four years ago along with his two sons."

Laura nodded. "It's a small world."

"Seems to be. Now, if there is nothing else you wish to discuss, I have a court engagement in half an hour."

Laura accepted the dismissal knowing how vexing it must have been for him to make an opening in his calendar for her. "Thank you, again, Mr. Dinford. I shall await your call."

He strode to the door and held it for her as she left his elegant office.

Her mind whirled with Dinford's up-coming handling of the estate. At least she was free of the bombshell.

* * * * *

She decided to stop in Moultrie and see Caper. As she walked to the shop several people nodded and smiled, including the police officer in the patrol car. She was warmed by the friendliness of the folks in Moultrie.

Again, she was greeted by the smiling sales woman, who nodded and went about her business. Laura went to the back of the shop and knocked on the office door. Caper called to come in and came to Laura as she entered.

"Been to see Dinford." It was a statement not a question.

"Yes."

"What did you think of him?"

"Very personable. Seems straight forward. He's going to take care of matters."

"Good! At least that relieves you of the burden." Caper returned to her desk and sat. "What are your plans for the rest of the day?"

"I haven't any."

"What say we go to the club for lunch?"

As usual, the club had its regular collection of women lunching in small groups. Laura noticed that Caper acknowledged a few as she strode behind Edmund to their table.

In an aside whisper, she said, "Guess they don't have much to do."

Laura gave an indifferent shrug, settled in her chair and glanced at the menu.

"How about a glass of wine." Caper asked.

"No, I think I'll just have iced tea."

Shirley, the waitress, came, took their orders and left.

Caper toyed with her napkin then looked directly at Laura. "Laura, what do you think of Patrick Ryan?"

The question was a surprise and Laura's eyes widened.

"I know I have no right to ask. It's just that I think you two would make a handsome couple."

"Really!" Laura didn't mean to sound so indignant then softened her voice and said, "He's okay, I guess. Haven't spent too much time with him. He seems to be busy."

"Yes, I guess he is. I understand he handles most of his business from his home."

Laura sipped her ice water. "That's what he told me. International business."

"He does go to Europe a couple of times a year. Amsterdam, Brussels, Africa..." Caper's voice drifted off, as in reflection of what she just said. "Must be exciting."

"I guess it could be if you're interested in travel."

"You're not?"

"Well, I haven't had much time to think about it. Been busy trying to make a living."

"Yeah, I know."

The wine stewardess brought the glass of Merlot for Caper, and Shirley, the waitress, placed their luncheon plates before them and Laura's iced tea.

While they ate, Laura told Caper of Ryan's unusual dinner arrangements on the past Friday evening and his repeated offer of buying.

Caper decided to hit Laura where she knew it would hurt. "Laura, I can't see you selling your mother's home. She loved it so. She spent many hours with the builders. It was something of a dream to her."

"Yes, I know. She always wanted a stone house, like they have in Pennsylvania."

"Yes, that's what she said. I think she drew the plans herself. Your father let her have her way when it came to the plans and building."

"Yes, Dad would do that." Tears sprung to Laura's eyes.

"I didn't mean to get you upset," Caper took Laura's hand and held it. "I thought the world of your mother. She was like my soul sister. When the house was under construction, your mother would take me out there and show me all the room consignments, the bathrooms, everything about the place."

They finished their lunch. Caper signed the club bill and they left, agreeing to get together soon.

On her way home, Laura decided to stop by Ryan's place. She determined that he made no introduction when he visited her parent's place, so she decided to turn the tables. She drove past her parents' place–now her home–and pulled into the driveway of ERIN.

The entrance to Patrick Ryan's residence was marked with tall stone columns. As she drove up the tree-lined drive she tried to catch a glimpse of the house but could not. On the last turn of the drive the residence was revealed in all its Georgian grandeur. A massive stone structure with three stories and possibly a full basement.

When she rang the chimes, the door was opened by Robert, who was delighted to see her.

"Miz Laura, how nice to see you again," His smiling face greeted her.

"Is Mr. Ryan in?," she asked.

"Yes, ma'am. I will fetch him immediately."

The butler led her into the living room and saw to her comfort before he left.

The room was elegantly furnished with handsome pieces of finest Chippendale, Queen Anne and Louis Quatorze interspersed with eclectic harmony. A Persian rug spread between two sofas making a warm conversational grouping. French doors were to the rear and she supposed they opened to a porch or patio. Laura sat on one sofa and waited for Patrick Ryan.

The clicking of toenails upon the oak flooring announced the arrival of Blarney as he scrambled before his master. Laura steeled herself for an onset but the dog walked over to her and rested his head upon her lap. She gingerly pet the huge head.

"That's enough Blarney. Go!"

The big dog obeyed and left the room.

Ryan faced Laura. "To what do I owe this pleasure?"

Laura squirmed then jutted out her chin. "I came to thank you for your help with Carleton Dinford." She noticed Ryan was casually dressed in gray slacks and a light gray golf shirt. The color emphasized his eyes. Steel gray. "I'm sorry if I interrupted you."

"I was about finished. I have to conduct my European business very early in the morning since they are hours ahead of us." He sat on the couch opposite Laura and gave her an askance look.

"I want to thank you for paving the way with Carleton Dinford. I know that without your introduction I would have had to wait some time before I got an appointment."

Ryan nodded his head. "I'm sure he was helpful."

"He will handle the, er, matter for me."

"Good! Now, would you like to see my operation room?"

Laura's eyes widened. "I beg your pardon?"

"Where I conduct all my business."

"Oh. I didn't know, at first, what you were referring to."

"Tsk, tsk. Laura, you have to change your opinion of me. I'm not a licentious person."

Laura's eyes hooded in disbelief. "Humph", she muttered, "when the cows come home."

Ryan shook his head, reached for her hand and led her out to the hall and to the back of the stairs. Laura dragged behind, hesitantly.

Much to her surprise she saw what appeared to be a singular elevator door.

"I had this put in when I built. It's quite handy. It does save Robert from having to come down three flights every day."

Laura's eyebrows rose. It was the first considerate thing she heard Patrick Ryan say.

The interior of the elevator was small, like a shower stall. When it passed the second floor, he said, "This is my bedroom level. I don't suppose you would want to see that," and he burst out laughing.

She could feel the heat flood her face. "Don't be ridiculous," she snapped.

When the elevator door opened she walked into a hallway much like that of the first floor. She noticed a sitting room, comfortably furnished and with a TV.

"These are Robert's and Mrs. Taylor's quarters." He pulled her toward the rear and opened the door. Laura gasped. The room was well lighted. A bank of computers filled one side of the room, and telephones, several, were beside each computer. On the wall above were several clocks ticking off the time around the world. It was like nothing she had ever seen.

"Well," she let out her breath, not realizing she had been holding it, and sighed, "I can see how you keep up with business and your clients."

"Everything here is of the latest, and when it becomes obsolete I replace it."

Laura walked about the room admiring the set-up and slid her hand over the printers and copiers. "Quite impressive."

"It should be. It represents a healthy sum of money."

"I can see that."

File cases lined another wall and a large library table sat in the middle of the room. Upon it were several letter trays filled with paperwork.

"Must keep you busy."

Ryan looked her in the eyes. "Not that busy."

Again Laura flushed. "I think you have a wonderful workplace, but I have to leave now."

"You mean you're not going to tell me how the meeting went with Dinford?"

She stared back at him, amazed at his gall. "I don't think it's any of your business, Mr Ryan."

"Laura, I thought we settled on our names. Please call me Patrick."

"Well, *Patrick*, please take me downstairs."

"Second floor or the first?"

Her mouth gaped open then snapped shut, her eyes tiny slits of loathing. "Really!"

Ryan chuckled. "Laura, when are you going to relax and cast off that prudish attitude?"

She stomped her way toward the door and down the hall toward the elevator. Ryan was close behind. They rode the lift down to the first floor and when the door opened Robert was standing there. He looked at Laura and then his employer but said nothing. He stepped aside to let Laura huff her way past.

Patrick Ryan took hold of Laura's hand and turned her about. "I didn't mean to be intrusive, Laura. I just want to be helpful."

"Well, if you want to be helpful, as you say, you'd better clean up your act." With that, Laura stormed out the front door which was being held open by a smiling Robert.

Ryan spun on his heel and headed into the living room toward the built-in bar.

Robert, still smiling, muttered. "Ump, ump, ump. I think you met your match, Mr. Pat."

CHAPTER 8

Laura slammed into the house, fumed into her father's den and poured herself a glass of Merlot.

"Just who does that man think he is, insinuating that I would be willing to have sex with him. Second floor, indeed."

She took a gulp of the red wine and dropped into her father's chair. Slowly, she rotated the glass until the bright red liquid covered the sides of the glass with its rainbow. She began to think how she could reciprocate his insulting remark. A plan formed in her mind. Carefully, she went over each detail to make sure it would work. Smiling, she picked up the phone and called Patrick Ryan.

"Miz Laura, I'm so glad you got home safely. You left in such a stew."

"Thank you, Robert, I was wondering if Mr. Ryan was available."

"Yes'am, I'll fetch him."

He came to the phone and sarcastically said, "Don't tell me you changed your mind."

Laura smirked, "Well, Patrick, in a way I have." She could hear the intake of his breath.

"Really?"

"Yes, really."

"Well, why not come here to dinner tonight?"

"Er, not tonight but how about tomorrow night?"

"Perfect. I'll pick you up about seven."

"No, I'll drive over myself. Seven o'clock, then," and she hung up before there could be any argument on his part. Now she had to enlist someone to make the call. Someone who could be exact, to the moment. She thought of calling one of her friends in Richmond, but the explanation or hassle she wanted to avoid. Sue Bader came to mind. She looked into her father's roll index cards and found the telephone number for the County Planning Commission. She dialed the number and Sue answered.

"Sue, this is Laura. I need your help."

"Anything, Laura, what can I do for you?"

"Can I meet you at George's tomorrow for lunch. I'll have all the timing worked tonight to give you."

Sue sounded baffled. "Ah, sounds like you're planning something. This reminds me of when Millie and I were working together on the exchange murders."

"Nothing that drastic. And if there is any murder committed, I'll be doing it."

Sue chuckled. "I've got to hear all this. Meet you tomorrow at George's. Bye," and she hung up the phone.

Laura took a writing pad from the drawer of her father's desk and titled the sheet:

TIMES.

7:00 Hor d'oeuvres (if any) time elapse, 20 minutes.

7:20-7:30 Dinner - time elapse 30 to 40 minutes. It is now somewhere around 9:00.

9:00 After-dinner drinks. CRUCIAL TIMING REQUIRED.

PRECISELY AT 9:30 call my number, my "call forwarding" will call Patrick Ryan's number and the butler will answer (I think), regardless, say you are from the law firm of Katz, Katz and Katz and must speak to Miss Laura Crowder. I will answer. Pay no attention to the gibberish I will say, but I will tell you, at the end, that this information is at the house and I will immediately go there to get it. At this point I will leave Ryan's place.

She set down the pen and softly laughed. *I think it just might work. He can cool off in the shower.*

She folded the paper and put it in her shoulder bag.

* * * * *

88

Thursday morning, Laura watched, as she did each morning since she was here, Patrick Ryan stride through the lower field with Blarney at his heels. She was familiar with his gate, the way he held his head, and admired his virility and stamina as he maintained a steady pace. Every time she watched him she would sigh remembering the feeling of his arms about her, carrying her to the patio and gently setting her down. She wanted to be out there with him, strolling through the woods line. Picking wild daisies. Breathing the fresh air. She shook her head. *Good Lord, what am I thinking, but he is quite handsome.*

She placed her cup and dish in the dishwasher and went upstairs to get ready to meet Sue Bader at noon.

* * * * *

George's was busy, as usual, and Laura scanned the room to find Sue Bader. The waving hand caught her eye and she went over and sat down at Sue's table.

"I couldn't sleep last night for thinking about what you want me to do," Sue said.

"I have it all written down, Sue. It's a matter of timing." She got out the folded sheet of paper.

Sue leaned over and looked Laura in the eyes. "First, I have to know just what it's all about. Is it legal?"

Laura laughed. "Yes, it's legal. It's just that I want to put Patrick Ryan in his place."

Sue's eyes widened. "You mean this has to do with Ryan?"

"Entirely."

The waitress took Laura's order, placed the glass of ice water before her, and left.

"Good golly, Miss Agnes."

Laura's brows raised. "I haven't heard that saying for some time now."

"Well, I tend to use the archaic expressions. Better than what you hear some people say."

The pre-prepared salad plate came along with the bill.

Laura handed the sheet of instructions to Sue, and while Sue perused it, Laura ate.

"I think I can handle this," Sue said, "but let me ask you a question, if I may. Just why do you want me to interrupt such a lovely evening? Or, as I'm beginning to think, you want to ward off his advances. Is that it?"

"Shrewd girl. You're exactly right." Laura told Sue about Patrick showing her the house and his *operation* room, his insinuating remark, and his put-down attitude toward her.

Sue nodded as she listened and finished her sandwich, then tucked the sheet of paper into her purse. "I'll do this for you on one condition."

Laura pulled up and frowned. "What's the 'condition'?"

"You gotta tell me all about it on Saturday."

The two giggling women caught the unwanted attention of some frowning customers.

"Guess I'd better get back to work." Sue reached over and took Laura's hand. "Thanks for having confidence in me. I won't let you down." She strode out of the restaurant and across the square to the County Administration Building.

Laura watched the retreating figure. *It's amazing that I do find confidence in Sue, knowing her such a short time.*

She paid her bill, drove to the strip mall where the supermarket was, and decided to check out the shops. The hair salon sign read WALK-INS WELCOME. Laura pushed open the door. A friendly voice greeted her.

"Come on in, I'm just about finished." She lightly hair-sprayed the gray haired woman, pulled off the apron covering her and shook it. "Thank you, Mrs. White. Same time next week?"

The elderly woman shook her head. "No, Cheryl, can't make it. We're having a special court session next week. I'll get in touch." With that, the woman passed the hairdresser some money and turned to leave.

Laura held out her hand, stopping the woman. "Did I hear you say 'court session'?"

"Yes. I'm the County Treasurer. I have to testify about certain records."

"Oh." Laura smiled with chagrin. "It just caught my attention because I am a lawyer."

The woman shoved out her hand. "I'm Margaret White. They call me Maggie."

Laura took her hand. "I'm Laura Crowder."

The gray hair woman looked closely at Laura. "Philip and Judith Crowder's daughter?"

Once more Laura was taken back by the grapevine of traveling information in this small town. "Yes, I am."

"You have my deepest sympathy, Miss Crowder. Your parents, even though they were newcomers to Moultrie, were very much liked and respected."

"Thank you," Laura managed through her tightening throat. "I appreciate your sentiments."

The town treasurer nodded and left.

The young hairdresser came up to Laura and studied her face. "Yes, I can see you have Judith's eyes." Giving the huge cover-up apron another shake, she said, "Now what can I do for you?"

"If you have the time, I'd like to have my hair washed and set."

"I have the time. Thursday isn't my busiest day."

While Cheryl Tanner, the hairdresser, washed Laura's hair she spun into her gentle discourse of her errant scanner and the news and conversations it picked up. Laura listened, fascinated by this discovery.

"I didn't know baby scanners could pick up outside phone conversations."

Cheryl Tanner went on to tell how she heard the two AAA messages; one from whom she thought was Amelia Talbot, and the other night, Sandra Perkins.

"Have you told the police about this?"

"I think my husband, Fred, reported it. Fred works for SCDOT at the district garage, and a volunteer fireman."

"I don't envy his volunteer job. Very hazardous."

* * * * *

Feeling quite cocky, Laura pranced into her home and bounced up the stairs to her bedroom. She planned to take a leisurely bath, with lots of bubbles, perfume her body to encourage Patrick Ryan's desire, then drop him coldly. She was certain her plan would work.

Her ablution completed, Laura chose the green silk dress from CAPER'S, slipped into it and stood before the cheval mirror to inspect the finished product. She fluffed her thick black hair, spread it over her shoulders and smiled.

Thinking of the line from the movie *Funny Girl* with Barbra Streisand, Laura sang , "Hey, Mr Ryan, here I come", and softly laughed.

The Mercedes purred up the long drive to ERIN and she parked at the front door. She got out carefully, brushed down the silk folds of the dress, marched to the door and rang the bell.

"Miz Crowder, it's so nice to see you", Robert said, flashing a bright white smile.

"Thank you, Robert. I trust Mr. Ryan is expecting me."

"Oh, yes ma'am, he's in the living room."

Laura, already being familiar with the layout of the house, strut into the living room, ready to turn on her charms.

A cool breeze came from the open French doors at the rear and beyond she could see a porch with wicker furniture. The paneled wall of the bar had been rolled back revealing its well stocked wares. Glasses had been set out and a bottle of Chardonnay. Ryan was sitting on the couch with his left foot wrapped and propped up on the far edge of the coffee table. A pained look on his face. Blarney, his golden Lab, lay at Ryan's right foot.

"Excuse me for not getting up," Ryan said.

Her intentions to excite Ryan deflated like a punctured tire.

"What happened to you?"

At the sound of her voice Blarney got up and went to Laura and she gingerly pat his head.

"I turned my ankle when I was out walking this morning,"

"Why didn't you call me and cancel the dinner arrangement?"

"Because I didn't want to cancel it."

She inspected the wrappings. "That looks professional."

"Dr. Lyon came from town and did the job."

"Dr. Lyon?"

"Yes, and he's also the county coroner. He diagnosed that I would live."

"I'm sure you will."

Laura's thoughts went to how he could be such a lover with one foot killing him. Not on a bet. She noticed his casual dress, his one Italian leather loafer, and his relaxed mood. His gray-blue eyes raked over her causing goose bumps on her arms.

"You look sensational," Patrick said.

She momentarily felt abashed. "Thank you."

"Will you do me a favor," and without waiting for her reply said, "get those two wine glasses on the bar and fill them for us."

Laura dropped her clutch purse on a chair and did as Patrick asked, noticing a bottle of Frangelico on the side and a phone behind the bar. She handed a glass to Ryan and, without any qualms, sat next to him on the couch. In his condition she felt safe.

"Sorry about your misfortune."

"So am I, but we can still enjoy the evening. Mrs. Taylor has gone to great lengths to prepare a very nice dinner."

Almost as if on cue, Robert walked into the room carrying a large tray. He set it on the coffee table, snapped his fingers and, with Blarney at his heels, left.

A delectable arrangements of small hors d'oeuvres were artistically arranged to encourage tasting and Laura needed no encouragement. She set her wine glass aside, picked up a small puff of pastry stuffed with shrimp filling and popped it into her mouth.

"Ummm, that's delicious."

"Yes, Mrs. Taylor is a gourmet cook. She's forever reading cook books or food magazines and trying out new recipes. I guess I should be thankful. No meal is dreary or a disaster."

Laura picked up another pastry and quickly finished it. "I can hardly wait to see what she has prepared for dinner."

Patrick Ryan set his wine glass on the side table, and struggled to try to move his foot from the coffee table. Laura jumped up and lifted it for him and gently set it down on the floor. She took a small plate, put two pastries on it and handed it to Ryan.

"I didn't know that your many talents included nursing."

"It's a built in, maternal instinct, thing."

"Well, it certainly was nice of you." He checked his watch. "We'll be dining soon."

The action brought to mind her devious plan for the evening. She peeked at her watch–7:28–and sighed. She could almost envision Sue Bader watching the clock, too.

"This is a very comfortably appointed room, much like my mother would design." The mention of her mother brought a tightness to her throat and she picked up her wine glass and sipped.

"I saw our similarity in furnishings when I was visiting Philip and Judith."

"Yes, as you said you were there many times."

"They held many parties, invited towns people, and, generally speaking, were well liked by the locals. Your mother was particularly fond of Caper Morgan, and your father seemed drawn to Pete Harris."

At the mention of Pete Harris, Laura felt her face flush and she quickly busied herself pretending to brush off crumbs from her lap. She felt she was in dangerous territory talking about her parents and she quickly changed the subject with the first thing that entered her mind.

"Patrick, what is your opinion on the missing women?"

Ryan gave her a questioning look, and shrugged. "I haven't given it much thought. They could be anywhere. Maybe they left the area."

"I don't think so. Both women had positions in town and I doubt they would just walk away."

"Well, until the sheriff finds further evidence to the contrary, such as foul play, I can only assume."

Robert stepped into the room. "Dinner is ready, Mr. Pat."

Ryan nodded, struggled to his feet and Laura stepped to his side and took his arm. The closeness of the man and the subtle aroma of his cologne or after-shave was physically exciting. She could feel the warmth of his body next to hers.

"Lean on me."

"Sounds like an old song I heard somewhere."

Laura smiled and nodded. "It does, doesn't it."

Together, they entered the dining room.

The table was set so Patrick was at the head and she was to his right. A colorful arrangement of flowers dominated the center of the table but was not overpowering. Laura guided Ryan to the head of the table and Robert held his chair as he sat. Then he quickly assisted Laura to her seat.

"Thank you, Robert."

"You're welcome, Miz Crowder."

Robert left the room and returned with the first course.

Laura steered the conversation to simple things, one was asking Ryan what it was like to walk in the woods.

Ryan was relaxed and very articulate when describing his jaunts, naming trees, vegetation and birds. She listened, watching the movements of his hands as he described his walks, and was mesmerized by his heavy dark eyebrows as they rose and fell with his dissertation. The evening passed quickly and with a sly peek at her watch Laura saw that it was 8:50.

Ryan caught her sneak-peek and asked, "Are you late for another appointment?"

Flustered, she stuttered, "No, no, of course not," and quickly added, "I was just thinking that maybe this evening was wearing on you. I know your foot must be aching."

"My dear Laura, I'll be the judge of my endurance. Shall we retire to the living room for after-dinner drinks."

It was not a question but a statement. Laura pushed back her chair and went to Ryan's side.

"Yes, I know, 'lean on me'. I appreciate your assistance."

Carefully, Laura led Patrick into the living room, once more experiencing her vibrations to his closeness as she helped him settle down where he previously had been. Without further instructions, Laura went to the wet bar, took two small glasses and poured the Frangelico, handing one to Ryan.

"Love this stuff," she said and took a slow sip then dropped down on the couch next to Patrick.

"Laura, tell me about your life in Richmond. Is there any one in particular that might be waiting for you?"

Unintentionally, she gave a deep sigh. "No, no one in particular."

"Do you rent or own your dwelling?"

"Rent, in a residential area called Baxter's Mill. It's a well established community started in the '70s. At the time I signed the lease, three years ago, I could not afford to buy or build."

"You could now. Is that what you want to do?"

Another deep sigh. "I don't really know what I want to do. First, I have to settle the estates, then I'll take it from there. I have been given a leave of absence from Katz et al in order to complete my business here."

Patrick reached out and took Laura's hand. "I know this was a horrible thing to drop on you, but from what I can see you can handle it."

His confidence in her ability was assuring and his touch was torment. She squirmed. "Yes, but it's going to take time and time is something I can't afford."

"Is that why you went to see Carleton Dinford?"

The question came out of the blue and put cold fear in her. She mulled on it and then decided to mince the truth. "Partially, after all he is familiar with South Carolina law, I'm not." She took another sip of Frangelico and in doing so managed to release her hand from his, afraid he could feel her racing pulse.

"You will find him a very capable attorney. Very discreet."

His steel gray eyes stared directly into hers as if he was searching for the answer to a riddle. Laura shifted in her seat feeling slightly uncomfortable under his hard gaze.

"I'm sure I will."

Laura was startled when the phone rang. Immediately she knew it was 9:30 and Sue Bader was following instructions.

In a few seconds Robert came to the living room entry and announced, "The phone call is for Miz Crowder from Katz, Katz and Katz."

Ryan, looking questioningly at Laura, pointed to the phone in the bar and Laura, mind whirling, got up and lifted the receiver.

"This is the law firm of Katz, Katz and Katz. Is this Miss Laura Crowder?"

"Yes, this is she."

"Well, now, how is the evening progressing?" Sue laughingly said.

"Yes, sir, I have those papers. They're in my briefcase."

"Sure, sure. I know. I'm not supposed to pay attention to your gibberish. Having a good time?"

"You must have the information tonight?"

"It's up to you. Do you really want to leave Patrick Ryan now?"

"I'll have to call you back. Yes, tonight. I should be able to call you in half an hour. Thank you," and Laura hung up the phone and turned toward Patrick Ryan. "I have to go home. I hope you don't mind. It's some information they need immediately for court papers in the morning."

"Really! I didn't think law firms worked at night."

"Sometimes it's necessary. Certain changes are made in briefs that have to be submitted to the courts."

"How did they know to call here?"

"I have call forwarding. I put your number in before I left."

"Oh." Patrick studied her face for a moment then smiled. "You were expecting the call?"

"Well, no, not exactly, it's a matter of habit." She gathered her purse. "It was a delightful evening, Patrick, and I thank you."

"I'm really sorry you have to leave so early. Things were just getting warmed up so to speak."

"Yes, but business is business. I'll call you in the morning to see how you are getting along."

Laura turned and left the living room leaving Patrick Ryan sitting on the couch.

Robert was in the foyer and quickly opened the front door for her.

"I sure hope everything was to your likin', Miz Crowder."

"Indeed it was, Robert, and please tell Mrs. Taylor that the Chicken Cordon Bleu was delicious."

"I will surely do that, Miz Crowder. She will appreciate knowing it."

"Goodnight, Robert."

Laura went to her car and drove home. She tossed her purse on the foyer table and went into her father's den and plopped down in the desk chair. Aloud, she said, "Now, Miss Smarty, what do you think you accomplish with that contrivance?" She sifted through the Rolodex for Sue's phone number, dialed and was greeted with a breathless voice.

"I'm anxious to hear what happened."

"Nothing happened. Actually, I was enjoying the evening."

"You were?"

"Yes, he was helpless. He turned his ankle and his foot was wrapped. A Dr. Lyon came from town to administer first aid."

"He's the local sawbones. I know of him," Sue replied.

"I do want to thank you for a job well done."

"Thanks. So, you were 'enjoying the evening'. I guess now you're regretting the farce."

"In a way I am, but then he got to asking personal questions. I guess it was time to leave."

"Still don't want him in your life?"

The question took Laura by surprise. She thought for a moment then said, "I don't know, Sue. I don't know if he's on the up-and-up or just playing me along."

"Patrick Ryan knows just what he is doing at all times. He's a very confident man. All business. I don't think he has time to play hanky-panky."

"You sound like you know him."

"Only through association. I watched him work his charms on Millie. But that's another story. Get some sleep and remember you promised to tell me all about it on Saturday. Do you want to meet me at George's?"

"How about you coming here, Sue. I'll fix lunch for us."

"Sounds good to me. I'll be there about 11:30. Bye."

Laura went up to her room, undressed and slipped into bed. She was a bit miffed with herself that her plan failed. She had hoped to get Ryan all hot and bothered but it never came about. As a matter of fact, he was quite nice. Amiable for a change. She confessed to herself that she was enjoying the evening until he started to ask questions.

She pulled her pillow down under her cheek and started to count sheep. It was going to be a long night.

CHAPTER 9

Friday morning she got out all the papers, policies, and stocks which she had brought from the bank lock box. It was going to be a long day writing letters to the insurance companies, sending death certificates, and her qualification certificates. She had to close out both her father's and mother's estates. She thought about Carleton Dinford who was probably doing the same thing on the insurance and stocks that were going to Peter Harris. She saved all the typed letters and information on 1.44 MB floppies, one for each estate.

Her back ached from strain and she shut down the computer.

The phone rang and she picked it up.

"Miss Crowder, this is Carleton Dinford. I just want you to know that I have written to the *beneficiary* (he stressed the word) to inform him that he has an anonymous benefactor and the necessary business transaction required by law includes personal information. I have asked him to call my office to make an appointment to come in with certain documents. If you wish, I will send you copies of our correspondence."

"No, no, Mr. Dinford, I do not wish to have any connection with the handling of that end of the estate. I have been advised by Mr. Ryan that you can handle it competently and discretely without my interference." *A little name-dropping wont hurt and obviously he is being discrete not using names over the phone.*

"Very well, Miss Crowder. I will take care of it completely."

"Thank you, Mr. Dinford. I appreciate that." She hung up the phone, got up, stretched, and headed for the front door.

Laura walked down to the mailbox and retrieved a copy of the *Moultrie Monitor*. The small weekly paper had an article on Sandra Perkins, the missing bank teller. Laura read the article carefully. The car had been found but there were no personal belongings, such as a purse, in the car.

"Strange. The details almost duplicate the previous missing woman, what was her name, the teacher, Amelia Talbot, yes, Talbot."

She dropped into her father's desk chair and spread the newspaper out on top of the desk. Swiveling the desk chair about, she reached for the wire waste basket beside the desk and pulled out last week's issue of the *Moultrie Monitor*. She cut out the article on Amelia Talbot and also Sandra Perkins.

Why would these two women voluntarily leave their car in the pitch black of the night? I would think they would feel safer inside the car unless someone they knew gave them a lift. That's a thought. Maybe someone went out there to pick them up. Someone? The killer? If it was the killer, how did he know they were stranded? I'm sure if I can think about the murders this way, the police can, too.

The phone rang again.

"Miz Crowder, this is Clifford Morris, the county appraiser. I was going over my records and I was wondering if you changed your mind about my appraising the estate of your parents?"

"No, Mr. Morris, I haven't made up my mind, as yet. I'm so sorry to sound *iffy* but I'll just have to take my time with my decisions. I hope you don't mind."

"No, not at all."

"I have your card. When I decide I will call you–one way or the other."

"That will be fine, Miz Crowder. Goodbye."

She replaced the phone in the cradle. A glance at her watch told her it was time for lunch.

* * * * *

After lunch she decided to call Patrick Ryan and he answered the phone.

"How is your ankle doing?"

"Kind of you to call and inquire. It's about the same, swollen and painful."

"Are you taking anything for the pain?"

"Yes, Dr. Lyon left me some pain-killers. I just took one."

"I know there is nothing I can do, but if there is please ask."

"Well now, since you asked, there is something you can do."

"What?"

"How about coming over this evening." and he quickly added, "just to chat and have a light supper? Robert and Mrs. Taylor are away this weekend visiting their South Carolina relatives and I'm miserable, and I'm helpless in the kitchen. I will get take-out from George's."

Laura thought about his situation and felt a twinge of remorse over her "best laid plans".

"Tell you what, how about my bringing over a picnic supper?"

"That sounds great. What time?"

"About seven."

"I can hardly wait."

She scrounged through the items in the refrigerator, remembering that she had invited Sue Bader to lunch tomorrow, and now her promising to bring a picnic supper to Ryan. She wanted to be innovative with the supper. *Why? Did she want to impress Ryan with her culinary skills?*

She pulled out the egg carton, took out enough eggs to boil for egg salad which would be the main item in tomorrow's lunch with Sue. But for Ryan? No, it was time to do some serious grocery shopping. As soon as the eggs boiled sufficiently, she covered the pan, shut off the stove and left.

At the supermarket she wandered through the aisles selecting various items of meat, fresh vegetables, and salad fixings. She resigned herself to the fact she would probably be here in South Carolina for at least two more weeks and shopped accordingly. A prickling sensation played at the back of her neck. Several times she turned about, having the feeling she was being watched. *Nah! Who would be watching me?*

She pushed the shopping cart to her car and was struggling to unload the groceries into the trunk.

"Here, let me help you, Miz Crowder."

Laura spun around and was facing a county police officer.

"Thank you. You're very kind." Realization struck her. "How did you know my name?"

"It's our business to know the newcomers in town. Please accept my sympathy for the loss of your father and mother."

His condolences surprised her. "Thank you."

He dropped the trunk lid, tipped his hat and strolled back to his patrol car.

At home, she put the groceries away, and assembled the ingredients for her "picnic supper" with Patrick Ryan. She determined not to compete with Mrs. Taylor. No way would she win. It would have to be a casserole. She checked her watch: 3:30. She took out the two large boneless chicken breasts, cut them in bite size pieces and sautéd them lightly. Put on a pot of white rice to which she added a sliced carrot. Chopped onions, green peppers and garlic. Removed the chicken from the skillet and sautéd the onions, peppers and garlic gently. Set them aside. Got out her mother's casserole dish, buttered it, and dumped in the cooked rice, carrots, onion, green pepper and garlic mix, mixing in a cupful of frozen peas, then scattered the chicken pieces over the top. Laura mixed all the ingredients just enough to make the mix interesting, adding several dashes of black pepper. She put four chicken bouillon cubes with two cups of water in the microwave to dissolve. When cool, she added two tablespoons of cornstarch, two tablespoons of soy sauce, and a few red pepper flakes, simmered the broth gently in the same skillet until just about thickened then stirred it into the chicken mix, topped it with panko, Japanese bread crumbs, and put it in the oven to bake for thirty or forty minutes. She then went up stairs to change her clothes–nothing fancy–her old college clothes would do.

At 6:30 she came down in her U of R sweatshirt and jeans. She sliced the French bread, buttered and seasoned the slices with garlic powder, then browned it under the broiler. The loaf was then wrapped in heavy aluminum to keep warm. The casserole dish was wrapped in several dish towels, and both were placed in a wicker hamper to carry. In a small plastic bowl she put some prepared salad fixings, sprinkled a few tablespoons of blue cheese and salad dressing atop, snapped the lid on and shook it. She put this in the basket along with a serving spoon for the casserole. She was on her way, feeling like Little Red Riding Hood about to meet the wolf. Albeit, a lame wolf.

* * * * *

She was about to ring the bell, changed her mind and cracked the front door, stuck her head in and called.

"Patrick, are you about?"

"Come in, come in. I'm in the living room."

Laura toted the basket into the living room and set it on the coffee table. The bar doors were rolled back revealing two wine glasses on the bar top and two bottles of wine; one red and one white. There were also two plates and what she perceived to be cutlery wrapped in linen napkins. She realized it must have been a painful effort for Ryan to assemble the items. Blarney, the golden retriever, was circling Laura's feet. She reached down and pat his big head, scratching him lightly behind the ears. The dog gave a pleasurable moan then returned to his master and settled at his one shod foot.

Patrick was wearing light tan slacks and a pull-over shirt. His foot was propped up on the coffee table again, but his face didn't register pain. His dark hair was uncombed and one stray lock dangled over his forehead. She thought he looked cute.

With a wave of his hand, he said, "Didn't know which one would be appropriate with your culinary endeavors."

"Actually, I don't adhere to the rule of white wine with fish and chicken, and red wine with red meats. It's all according to how I feel."

She poured two glasses of the white wine and handed one to Ryan.

"And just how do you feel?"

"Actually, I feel pretty good. Quite smug. I haven't cooked a meal for anyone for some time, now, so I hope it's to your liking."

"Not to worry, I'm easy to please–that is–when it comes to food."

Laura felt her pulse jump. *The man's a rogue. He's already casting the fish line. I'll fix you, Mr. Ryan.*

"Well, then, my casserole should satisfy you." *Oh no! I shouldn't have used that word, he's grinning.*

"We shall see how *satisfied* I get." His steel gray eyes swept over her face. "Is it all right with you if we dine here?"

"Yes, yes, of course. I didn't fix anything drippy."

"I'm anxious to see what you did fix."

"I'm not going to say it isn't much, it is. I'm not accustomed to cooking for two, just one."

"I'm very happy that you came to my rescue. Now, how about serving your 'picnic dinner'."

"Coming up."

She got the plates from the bar, uncovered her dishes, filled the plates, including the salad and a slice of warm French bread,, and handed one to Patrick along with a wrapped napkin holding silverware.

"Smells delicious. You're hiding your light under a bushel."

"We'll see," she mumbled as she served her own plate and sat next to Patrick. Her first taste was acceptable, and she took another fork full. She noticed Patrick was enjoying his meal. *A success.*

"I know you don't have all this stored in your refrigerator, did you shop this afternoon?"

"As a matter of fact, I did. Went to the supermarket. Your friendly constable of police helped me load the groceries in my trunk."

"Who was that?"

"I don't know. I haven't been personally introduced. But he had a nice smile. Had a patch over his cheek."

"Must have been Officer Clark. He's the one that had the run-in with the illegal and a knife."

They finished their meal, and much to Laura's appreciation Patrick finished everything. *He must have been hungry.*

"I didn't fix any dessert."

"Well, if you would be so kind, go into the kitchen, in the refrigerator, and you will find a Boston Cream Pie that Mrs. Taylor fixed before she left."

Laura walked across the hall, through the dining room and into the kitchen. She stopped and was awe-struck. The kitchen was huge. A six burner *Viking* range, side-by-side *Sub*-Zero freezer and refrigerator, and yards of counter space, including a work island four feet wide and about eight feet long.

Aloud, she said, "This is what keeps Mrs. Taylor happy."

She found the pie, looked for some dishes and a knife to cut it, and brought the pie in to Ryan.

"What a great kitchen you have."

"Mrs. Taylor drew up the specifications for the kitchen. She knew what she wanted."

"She is a woman of many talents," Laura said.

Just as they began to eat the pie, the door bell rang.

"Who in the hell is that?"

"I'll go see."

Laura opened the door and met the face of Butler Brown, the attorney.

"I'm sorry to intrude," he smiled, his eyes raking over Laura, "Miss Crowder, but I must talk to Ryan."

"Come in, come in. You're just in time for a piece of pie."

Brown went into the living room needing no directions. He was familiar with the house.

"Ryan, I heard you were laid up with a hurt foot, but I have to discuss something with you. I'm sorry for the intrusion." He glanced back at Laura, taking in her informal dress. then settled his ponderous body into a wing chair at the end of the couch.

"It's fine. We finished our supper. Would you like to have a piece of pie? Laura, get BB a piece of pie."

It sounded like an order, and she raised her eyebrows.

"If you don't mind," he added.

Laura went back into the kitchen, cut another slice of pie, got another fork, brought it into the living room, and handed it to Butler Brown.

He greedily accepted it. It took only a few fork-fulls for him to finish the pie. Setting the plate aside, he said, "Ryan, I have to discuss something with you, something of importance." He gave a fleeting glance at Laura.

"What ever you have to say to me, you can say in Laura's presence."

Laura pulled herself straight. It was an admittance of complete trust in her and she felt herself blush.

"I can go into the kitchen if it's a private conversation."

"No way! What he has to say, he can say in front of you."

She snuggled lower into the couch cushions, trying to make herself inconspicuous.

"Ryan, these women that are missing, I talked to Sheriff Melichampe, and he thinks the incidents may be related." He glanced at Laura, who was trying not to listen, then back at Patrick Ryan, "There are too many similarities."

Ryan pulled himself upright. "What's that got to do with me?"

"Well, we thought we could bring in an outsider. A private detective, to snoop around, and we thought you might help us locate one. Someone far out of town, like New York. Before you know it, SLED will be moving in and taking over."

Laura straightened. "SLED?"

"South Carolina's State Law Enforcement Division, and we don't want them poking around."

"Did Sheriff Melichampe discuss the possibility that perhaps someone these women knew came out to pick them up?", Laura added.

Butler Brown looked surprised. "He did say there was a possibility."

"I thought of that myself. There's no way these women would leave the safety of their car to venture out in the night, alone. It had to be someone they trusted. Or, thought they could trust."

Ryan wiggled around on the couch cushions. "I do know a very good investigator. Used to work for the city, now semi-retired. I had occasion to use his services in New York."

Laura gave him a questioning glance.

"Diamonds. Some people like to acquire them illegally."

Laura nodded.

"If you want me to, I can give him a call, but I can tell you his services are not cheap, a per diem of several hundred dollars plus expenses."

"Let me give Mellichampe a call." Butler Brown walked to the bar phone and punched in the numbers.

Across the room, and with his back turned, it was not easy to hear his conversation with the sheriff, so Laura faced Ryan.

"I was of the same opinion. A serial killer. If this gets out the women of this county are going to get paranoid. They'll be buying guns."

"Don't get your dander up, Laura. I'm sure Sheriff Mellichampe will keep this info under wraps."

"I don't think that's fair, either. He should put a notice in the paper advising women to be especially careful when driving at night."

Brown turned toward them. "He said that funds would be appropriated for the investigator's charges and expenses. Mellichampe must have discussed this with the mayor before he approached me."

"I'll make the call. Of course, it depends on whether he is working on a case or not. I'll call him in the morning and then call you."

Butler Brown nodded and turned to leave. "Thanks, Ryan, I'll wait to hear from you." Turning to Laura he said, "And thank you, Miss Crowder, for the pie, it was delicious."

After Brown left, Laura gathered up her casserole dish and remains of their meal and put it in the wicker hamper.

"Don't tell me you're leaving. You didn't get a phone call tonight."

Laura could feel her face flush. "I'm sorry about that, Patrick, but business is business. Besides, it's getting late."

"You're right, Laura. I do appreciate all your efforts preparing the meal. I'd have starved to death if you didn't come to my rescue."

Laura gave a slight laugh. "I don't think so, Patrick, remember, I looked into your refrigerator. It seems more than adequately stocked." She saw the glint of amusement in his gray eyes.

Ryan grinned. "Yes, I know, but I just wanted to have your company. I need your company, Laura. Will you kiss me goodnight."

She bent down and gave Patrick a kiss on his lips. Her lips tingled with his returned kiss. "I'm glad you didn't add 'and tuck me in'."

Ryan threw back his head and laughed. It was a contagious laugh and Laura laughed with him.

She gathered up the basket. "I'll call you in the morning, Patrick."

CHAPTER 10

Saturday was a beautiful day. The morning sunshine splintered its rays through the horizontal blinds of the bedroom. Laura stretched and got up. After her shower she got into a pair of jeans and T-shirt and went downstairs into the kitchen. She looked out the window above the sink and studied the woods line. *I know he must be missing his walk. Blarney, too. Maybe I'll go over there sometime this afternoon and take Blarney for a walk.*

She pulled back, astonished at how her thoughts have changed in two short weeks. She shook her head in disbelief.

After her coffee, she started to prepare the makings for a salad plate for Sue and herself. It would be a simple salad plate. Egg salad on a bed of crisp iceberg lettuce bordered with sliced tomatoes. Imitation crab meat (*surimi*) and salad shrimp mixed with a bit of onion, green pepper, and mayonnaise. A jug of iced tea. That's it!

She poured herself another cup of coffee and went out on the patio to sit. The light breeze gusted with the delicate aroma of fresh growth. An earthy smell came from the woods across the field. The bright spring green of new leaves sparkled and glinted in the morning sunlight. *Glinted? What could glint so sharply?* She finished her coffee, checked her watch, and went inside to prepare the luncheon plates.

Sue was prompt, arriving at 11:30. She whirled through the door, effervescent and chatty.

"I gotta hear everything. I can't believe you wanted to leave him high and dry."

"Whoa! Slow down! Let's get our plates and go out on the patio. I can tell you all about it while we eat."

"Sounds good to me."

Laura pulled the two prepared plates from the fridge, handed one to Sue, grabbed the iced tea jug, and led the way out to the patio. The patio table had been set with the necessary condiments, silverware, napkins, and iced tea glasses before Sue arrived.

The two women settled into the chairs.

"Gosh, this looks great." Sue flipped open her napkin and picked up her fork. "Since I'm here to listen, I'll eat and you tell me why you had to leave your handsome neighbor." She dug into the seafood salad and munched.

"Well, as it turned out. I really didn't have to leave my 'handsome neighbor'. When I got there, Patrick..." Laura noticed Sue's eyebrow raise. "We're on first name basis, of course."

"Of course," Sue nodded.

"Well, he had his left foot wrapped and on top the coffee table."

Both Sue's eyebrows raised.

"As I told you on the phone Thursday night, he turned his ankle when he went for a walk in the woods that morning. Dr. Lyon, the local *sawbones* as you call him, took care of Patrick."

Sue was nodding her head as she listened and indicating with her fork to go on. Her mouth was too full to speak. Laura was both amused and glad the luncheon pleased her.

"Mrs. Taylor, Patrick's housekeeper and chef *accompli* made delicious hor d'oeuvres, dinner, and dessert."

Sue smiled. "From soup to nuts."

Laura grinned. "Exactly. We were having after dinner drinks when you placed the call."

"So, tell me, why didn't you just ignore your intention and stay?"

"Well, Patrick was asking some personal questions..." Laura stopped. She didn't want to go into the questions with Sue.

Sue read Laura's face. "Oh, well, he got a bit nosey. I'm sure he only meant to converse. But, then again, he might have been diggin' to see if you had a beau waiting in Richmond."

"I'm sure that was what he was doing."

"Do you have a beau?"

"No. Anyway, I had a wonderful evening, and Friday morning I called him. He said the Taylors were off this weekend and so I took him a picnic supper last night."

Sue's eyebrows rose again.

"He was going to call George's for take-out. I told him I'd make something, and I did. A chicken casserole."

Sue nodded. "Better eat your lunch. I'll talk for a while."

Laura took a fork-full of the seafood salad and found it quite delicious.

"There's a buzz goin' around town about the two missing women."

"What's it about?"

"Seems the sheriff visited the mayor, spent some time in his office, then left. Word is, they talked about the two missing women, Amelia Talbot and Sandra Perkins."

Laura could not divulge the fact that Butler Brown spoke with Patrick Friday night about the same matter.

"Do you know what's going on?"

"No, but it wont be long and the drift of their conversation will leak."

Laura refilled their iced tea glasses. "Do you think they have a suspect?"

"I don't think so. Somethin' like that would be hard to keep under wraps."

They both nodded, finished their lunch and collected their plates and glasses to carry to the kitchen.

"Thank you, Laura, it was a delicious lunch. Can I help you clean up?"

"No, I'll put them in the dishwasher. Don't tell me you're hurrying off?"

"Yep! Got a date with Pete tonight. We're goin' out to have dinner then to the Abbeville Opera House to see a play."

At the mention of Pete's name, Laura pulled back. "Oh, well, sounds wonderful." She frowned. "Opera House? A play?"

"Yes, the old Opera House now offers plays and a lot of the actors are local citizens. They do a great job." Sue picked up her purse. "Are ya sure I can't help you clean up?"

"Thanks, but no. I can take care of it."

With a wave of her hand, Sue left.

* * * * *

At 3:30 the phone rang.

"Don't suppose you could do a repeat performance tonight, could you?"

"You mean fix another picnic dinner?"

"No, I mean come over and spend some time with me. I'm lonely."

"Have you had anything to eat today?"

"A piece of pie."

"Patrick, that's not enough."

"Well, I have no culinary experience except on the eating end."

"When I was nosing around in your kitchen I saw lots of possibilities in your fridge."

"Would you come over later and conjure up the possibilities for this starving man?"

Laura gave a light laugh. "Starving, indeed." She thought for a minute then said, "Yes, I'll be over about 5:30 to see what I can whip up."

"'Whip' is a harsh word. How about stir up?"

"Whatever, Patrick. See you then."

* * * * *

"Look, Patrick, Mrs. Taylor has a package of Italian sausage in here." Laura took out the sausage. "I can make some spaghetti and use these in the sauce."

Ryan, with the use of a cane, shuffled over and peered over her shoulder. "Sounds fine with me. I thought it took hours to cook spaghetti sauce."

"Not for me. I'm not a traditionalist when it comes to cooking."

"Would you mind if I sat here in the kitchen and watched you?" Seeing her frown, he added, "I might learn something for future use."

Laura gave an indifferent shrug and began looking for canned tomatoes, onions, and other necessities. She found the pantry generously stocked. She looked down the shelves of supplies. *I could have a field day making dinners. Everything you could possibly need is at your fingertips.*

"Where's Blarney?"

"He's out on the porch. He's been fed. It's just me that's starving."

Laura laughed and she saw the grin on Patrick's handsome face. A lock of dark hair fell over his forehead. And she thought how cute he looked. She opened the cabinet doors, found a stock pot to cook the spaghetti in, a saucepan for the tomato sauce, and went to work making her version of Italian spaghetti sauce. Patrick sat quietly watching her every move. When the sauce was simmering she said, "How about a glass of *vino* while I'm cooking?"

"Excellent idea." Ryan got up and shuffled out of the kitchen. In a few minutes he was back with a bottle of Merlot. "Couldn't carry the glasses. I think there are some here in the kitchen."

Laura opened cupboard doors until she found one with glasses. "These will do." She placed two balloon glasses on the table and Patrick filled them. She sat opposite him and held up her glass in a toast. "Here's to the dinner however it may be."

Ryan grinned, clinked his glass to hers and they sipped their wine. "Since we're playing house..."

"Yessss?" Laura's voice rose with inquiry.

"I thought it might be nice if we discussed future plans."

"Patrick, I haven't got the foggiest as to what I'll be doing in the future."

"You should be thinking about your future, Laura. You know 'time and tide waits for no man'."

"Are you saying that I'd better hurry up or I'll find myself a spinster?"

"No such thing! I was thinking of myself in that thought. After all, Laura, I'm 45."

"Well, what do you want me to do about that?"

"You know I'm extremely fond of you. At least, you should know. I've made a simpering ass of myself doting over you."

"I hadn't noticed." she lied. She had felt their vibes ever since they first met.

"I'll be a little old fashion. Would you mind if I court you?"

"Why, Mr. Ryan," she purred, "how chivalrous of you. I would have thought you were the kind that just reached out and took what you wanted."

"Normally, that's what I would do, but in your case, it would not work. I learned my lesson on that."

Coyly, Laura said, "With Millie?"

Patrick Ryan pulled up short. "Who's been telling you about Millie?"

"I heard it from a friend." Laura saw his discomfort. "I didn't mean to pry."

Yes you did, but that's long past. I suppose you've been talking to Sue Bader. She was Millie's friend."

"Yes, as a matter of fact she told me Millie married a reporter from Harrisonburg, Virginia."

"Yes, she did, and from what I hear, she is very happy. I probably would have made her miserable."

"Why do you say that?"

"We were not exactly compatible."

"And you think we are?"

"Oh yes. I think we are very compatible."

And why do you say that. You hardly know me."

"Because you don't take any crap, if you'll excuse my French."

Laura lifted her chin and laughed. "You got that right, Mr. Ryan." She lifted her glass, tipped it toward him, and sipped the wine.

Patrick Ryan looked directly into Laura's eyes. "I never did find out if there was someone waiting in Richmond but I don't care." He lifted his glass, tipped it toward Laura and said, "Here's to us", and sipped his wine.

She complied by nodding and sipping the wine. She set her glass down, got up and stirred the sauce, lifted the lid on the pot to boiling water and put the spaghetti in, got out two plates, the necessary silverware, and turned to Ryan. "Would you mind too much if we dined in the kitchen? It will save a lot of carrying to the dining room."

"Fine with me. It would also save me from shuffling into the other room."

Laura realized it must have been painful for Patrick to get the wine. "I should have thought of that when I asked you to get wine. Hereafter, just tell me where it is and I'll get it."

She checked the sauce and spaghetti, considered them done. Served the drained spaghetti, placed two sausages on each plate and covered the pasta with sauce. Grated parmesan cheese topped the rendition. "I didn't ask if you wanted a salad."

"No, this is fine." After tasting the spaghetti sauce, Ryan said, "This is pretty good for being quickly made."

"Think nothing of it, Mr. Ryan, I'm just full of those quick tricks." Again, she thought her words were suggestive and quickly added, "I have to make most of my own meals in short order. I don't have much time to spare."

"You are one accomplished woman." Ryan reached over and covered her hand with his.

Laura was tempted to pull hers back but changed her mind. It felt so very nice under his. *After all, he did say he wanted to "court" me.*

"When will Robert and Mrs. Taylor be home?"

"Tomorrow evening."

They finished their meal and he refilled the wine glasses.

"I called my friend in New York as I promised BB. He's not working a case at this time so he said he would take this one on. He will be in contact with me when he arrives in Moultrie but he'll do it in his own way and time. I'll know when he's here when he contacts me."

Laura raised her eyebrows. "Everything *sub rosa*."

"Exactly. No one will know he's here, least of all the sheriff's men. He likes to work alone."

"He might get into trouble going it alone."

"No, I don't think so. He just doesn't want anyone under foot."

"How will he get the police reports if he doesn't go to the sheriff's office?"

"He'll pick up his information wherever. He'll work through the back door, so to speak."

"Patrick, tell this gentleman that I heard something interesting at the beauty parlor." She saw Patrick's eyes widen, and said, "I had my hair washed." He nodded, and she went on. "The owner of the shop, Cheryl Tanner, said that her baby scanner picked up phone conversations. She told me that she heard the two phone calls to the AAA, one from the first missing woman, Amelia Taylor, and the other from Sandra Perkins."

"I'll be sure to tell him. It will give him a lead."

Laura gathered the dishes, rinsed and put them in the dishwasher, and sat back down at the kitchen table.

"Patrick, I still haven't made up my mind about selling."

"Don't!" Ryan said emphatically, "I don't want to court you long distance. Besides, when we marry you will live here."

"Marry!" Laura's jaw dropped.

"Of course. It's the purpose of my courtship. Is it so repulsive to you?"

"Marry. I haven't given marriage a thought."

"Well, my dear Laura, my intentions are honorable."

"You're rushing me, Patrick."

"I think I have to. I don't want you to go back to Richmond. I want you here, with me."

Laura could feel the flush spread over her face. "I guess that's your aggressive side showing up."

He took her hand, raised it to his lips and softly kissed it. "Do you mind if I am aggressive when it comes to you?"

"Just remember, as you said, I don't take any crap. I'm straight to the point."

"Good! So am I. Consider yourself engaged. I will present you with an engagement ring as soon as I can."

Laura stood. "I think I'd better leave now. I have some thinking to do."

"Make sure it's all positive. You know *the power of positive thinking*. I want you to be positive of your decision."

"You know, Ryan, you haven't even told me that you loved me."

"If I were physically able, at this time, I would sweep you off your feet, carry you upstairs, and make passionate love to you."

Laura could feel her blush deepen. His handsome face was both serious and lecherous. To lighten the moment she said, "Must be the spaghetti dinner."

Patrick Ryan threw back his head and laughed, a deep, loud laugh.

Laura broke into a grin and laughed along with him. "I'll call you tomorrow," and she left.

CHAPTER 11

Monday afternoon, a tall, muscular black man casually walked past the shop fronts along the town square of Moultrie. A camera was strung around his neck and a tourist guide in his hand. His quick, cold eyes took in every male person who past, ran them through his mental mug shots, and discarded their image from his memory. No match. A tough job lay before him. However, he promised Patrick Ryan he'd take it on.

He stepped into George's restaurant, asked about a public telephone, and was led to one outside the restrooms. He dialed the number from memory.

"Ryan's residence," came the quick reply.

"Mr. Ryan, please."

"Who shall I say is callin'?"

"Please tell him it's his New York friend."

"One moment, please," Robert said, and went to carry the bar phone to his employer.

"Ryan here."

"Mr. Ryan, got into town late last night. Staying with an old 'Nam army buddy of mine."

"You were quick to get here. I won't ask who the 'army buddy' is because I'd probably know him."

"I'd like to meet with you, go over some info I got from my buddy, and hear what you have to say."

"Come to the house tonight, around 10:00, I have some information, too, that might be useful. Did you fly or drive?"

"Flew. Got a rental."

"I live out on Route 57 west."

"I know where you live."

"Your army buddy?"

"Yep! See you at 10:00"

Robert's eyes widened as he recognized the visitor.

"Good to see you, again, Mr. Jackson."

"You, too, Robert. Been a long time. Thank you for remembering me."

"Always 'member persons of importance."

The tall black investigator snickered. "Importance. Huh! I'm just a retired policeman looking for work."

Robert shook his head. "Never that, Mr. Jackson. Please come this way," and led Jackson into the living room where Patrick Ryan greeted his visitor warmly but remained sitting on the couch with his left foot propped on the coffee table.

"What the hell happened to you?" Roger Jackson asked.

"Had a mishap with a rock when out strolling in the woods. How have you been, Roger? It's been a couple of months since I last saw you in New York. Keeping busy?"

"Try to. In between when you called. Glad to get the assignment."

"What can I fix you to drink?"

"Bourbon and branch."

Patrick Ryan nodded to Robert. "I'll have my usual."

Robert turned toward the bar and began to fix the drinks."

Jackson said, "Your usual?"

"Glenlivet scotch with a dash of soda.." He studied the tall black man. The tailor-made suit fit him perfectly. There was just enough tailoring ease under his left arm to accommodate his gun holster. "You're looking good, Roger, life must be treating you well."

"Can't complain. Chief even calls me on some cases. Sticky ones. I manage."

"And pretty well from the looks of you. I like your suit."

"Hey, coming from you, I'll take that as an extreme complement."

Robert chuckled. "If I may say so, Mr. Jackson, Y'all haven't changed a bit." .

The three men laughed together.

Robert handed the drinks to the two men and said, "If there's nothin' else, Mr. Pat, I'll retire."

"You go ahead, Robert, Mr. Jackson and I have business to discuss."

With a nod, Robert left.

Jackson and Ryan sipped their drinks and relaxed back into the cushions of the sofa.

Jackson said, "I've talked to my army buddy. He tells me two women are missing. Amelia Talbot and Sandra Perkins. Two women with positions in the community. Most likely not run-aways. From what I hear from my buddy, the families are greatly upset at their disappearance. I'll make the opportunity to talk to the families, someway, and find out what they think. These young women all disappeared due to car failure. Seems strange they'd leave their car in the dead of night."

"That's what my...financée said."

"Your financée? Thinking of getting married again."

The "again" shook Ryan. "It's been a few years since I've been married, Jackson. You should know that."

"I do, I did all the investigative work for you."

"Well, don't you think this ol' man should settle down again?"

"Hey, more power to you. I hope I meet her."

"You will. She owns the property next door. Her name is Laura Crowder, she is an attorney from Richmond. Long story."

"All right, let's talk about why I'm here."

"Jackson, Laura told me that her hairdresser, Cheryl Tanner, has a baby scanner that mysteriously picks up cell phone calls. Don't ask me how this happens, but Tanner heard both calls to the AAA from the women's cell phones."

"Yes, I'm familiar with this. Washington is picking up all cell phone calls on their "Big Daddy" monitor, not to mention monitoring e-mails."

"Tanner's husband, Fred, is a volunteer fireman in town."

"Bless his heart. That's a nasty job."

"Well he knows about the scanner and what it picks up. He also has a police scanner in his home."

"I'd think so, with his job. So, we're saying that the distress calls were from cell phones placed by each of the two women."

"Yes."

"Boy, that makes the range wider than I expected. What I have to do is find out how many baby scanners there are in Moultrie, South Carolina." Jackson took out a small note pad and starting writing. *Tanner. Hairdresser. Baby scanner. Fireman.*

"What do you think you'll do next, Roger?"

"Library work."

"Yes, I remember. You have my number. Keep in touch." Ryan settled back. "How's the family? Kids doing okay?"

"Couldn't be better. Lorine is taking night classes. Wants to improve herself. She's a pistol."

"Same Lorine I remember. I think someday she'll run for politics."

"Could be, but not as long as I'm alive. Politics, huh! Bunch of crooks."

Ryan laughed.

Roger Jackson got up, nodded at Ryan, and left.

* * * * *

Laura called Ryan early Tuesday morning.

"Do you think Blarney would walk with me in the woods?"

"I think he'd be ecstatic. Come over and have a cup of coffee with me."

"I'll be there in a few minutes." She looked down at her crumpled jeans and gave a shrug. *Who'll notice?*

This time, Laura rang the bell knowing Robert would be answering the door.

"Morning Miz Crowder. Mr. Pat is in the living room. I'll bring in your coffee."

"Thank you, Robert."

Laura proceeded into the living room and found Ryan in almost the same position as when she left Saturday night. Blarney got up wagging his tail, greeted her, then after she pet him he went back and lay down next to Ryan's foot.

"Do you sleep in this room? You're in exactly the same position as when I left the other night."

"No, I don't sleep here, I have a bedroom. I just stay here most of the day. It makes it easier for Robert."

Again, she was reminded of Patrick's concern for his servant. "Yes, I guess it would be."

He patted the cushion next to him and she sat where he indicated. Robert came in, placed the small tray on the coffee table and left. Laura picked up her cup of coffee and sipped.

"Laura, you haven't been out in those woods and are not familiar with the trail. It's an old logging road. The trail is clearly broken and well worn but don't go off it. You could become 'turned around'."

"You mean lost?"

"Yes. I only wish I could go with you."

"I do, too." The words were out of her mouth before she realized it.

Patrick's gray eyes grew serious. "Do you?"

Laura recovered from her slip-of-the-tongue. "I like company to talk to, and you could tell me, again, about the trees and other *flora* and *fauna*."

"I really would like that, too."

She put her cup back on the tray. "Will Blarney be a problem? Does he mind?"

"You'll have no trouble with him." Ryan reached to his side, picked up the leash and handed it to Laura. "You really don't need this. He'll run through the fields but when he gets to the woods he'll stay with you."

Blarney got up and went to Laura. She attached the leash to his collar and headed toward the French doors. "I won't be long. It's my first excursion into the woods so I won't go far."

Laura walked out the back, down the stairs of the porch, and headed for the woods. She could plainly see the path Patrick referred to. Blarney kept to her side, glancing every once in a while at her. She reached down and unlatched the leash. Blarney took off, leaping through the field straw, and circling Laura.

She followed the worn path into the woods back behind her home and was enjoying the stroll. She saw the overgrown logging road. It was still wide enough to accommodate a truck. She came upon a small clearing down from her own patio and saw that someone had been there. Cigarette butts were crushed out and dropped on the ground. Blarney sniffed at them, and sneezed, as if to point them out.

Wonder who was here. Patrick doesn't smoke, at least not that I've seen.

She walked a bit further and saw that the logging road crossed a stream. On the other side she could make out the imprint of tires in the soft mud.

Blarney went to the road side, squatted down and did his business, then was eager to return to the house. Laura obliged.

Back at ERIN, Blarney headed for the kitchen. Laura strode into the living room and frowned at Ryan.

"Patrick, do you smoke?"

"Hell, no! What gave you that idea?" Patrick pulled himself upright and stared at her.

"When I was in the woods behind my home I found crushed out cigarette butts on the ground in a clearing. I was wondering if you left them there."

"Cigarette butts? No one is supposed to be out there. It's private property. Smoking in the woods could be dangerous. Cause a woods fire."

"I know. Is anyone allowed to walk or drive through?"

"No one." Ryan frowned. "Drive through?"

"I saw tire tracks on the other side of the stream. Where does the logging road go?"

"To a county road that borders the back of our properties, and cuts across north of Moultrie."

"Strange. Someone has been out there."

"I'll have to report this to the sheriff. Don't want any trespassers."

"When I was on my patio the other day I saw the sharp flash of metal or glass reflected by the sun. I didn't pay much attention to it, but now, I'm sure someone was in that clearing. Maybe a couple of young lovers."

"Possibly, but I doubt it. Moultrie has its own 'lover's lane', so to speak." He saw Laura's eyebrows rise. "Or so I understand from Sheriff Mellichampe."

"Well, I have to run. I'll give you a call later to see how you are doing," and she left.

* * * * *

The New York investigator, Roger Jackson, sat opposite his 'Nam army buddy, Charles Godwin, while his wife, Joellyn, made breakfast.

"So," Godwin said in his deep resonant voice, "you've been hired to look into the disappearance of the two missing women."

"Yes, but I can't say much and you know that."

"Yes, I do and I respect your silence. As I told you, I only know what I've heard and what I read."

"Yeah. It's going to be tough. I have to go to the library and read the accounts, then, if possible, I'll visit the families."

"I know both families and I will give you a letter of introduction. If they are so inclined they will tell you what they know."

"That sounds good to me," Jackson said.

Joellyn placed the platter of eggs, bacon, and toast on the table. "You need a good breakfast to begin the day. I have plenty of coffee to go with it." She gave Jackson her best smile. "And a bowl of grits."

Roger Jackson looked into Joellyn's eyes and said, "You cook like my wife, and I thank you."

Joellyn puffed with the complement. "Thank *you.*"

Later that morning, after receiving directions to the library, Carter entered the brick building, went down the aisle between the stacks, and found the racks of newspapers. He slipped through the current issues and found the reports on the first missing person, Amelia Talbot. He read the column, then found the next issue that reported the missing of Sandra Perkins. He took out his note pad, jotted down pertinent facts, and nodded at the similarity.

Has to be the same guy. Guy? Yes, a man, someone the women knew. Trusted. I have to read the police reports. How can I get them?

* * * * *

"I said I'd call to see how you were doing."

"I'm doing fine. Dr. Lyon is here, re-wrapping my foot. Says it looks good. Swelling has gone down. I should be up and about in no time."

"Wonderful! I know Robert and Mrs. Taylor are taking good care of you so I won't worry."

"Were you worried, Laura?"

She drew in a breath then released it slowly, realizing the truth. "Of course I was, Patrick. It won't be long before we can dine at the country club."

"Excellent idea, Laura. I can hardly wait."

She hung up the phone. *Laura Crowder, you're heading for trouble. You want to find out what he means by "courtship".*

CHAPTER 12

From his parked rental car, he studied the outside of the building carefully. He watched the three deputies come and go wondering if the force had a night shift. The three deputies left around 6:00, in their private vehicles, just as the side parking lot lights came on.

Jackson, clad in black, got out of the dark blue rental, crossed the street and walked around the building. *Piece of cake.* The back of the building was in darkness. No lights. Not even one over the rear entrance.

He took out his ID card, ran it past the door lock tumbler and gently pushed. The door opened. Quietly, he slipped into the hall and noted the old wooden flooring. No carpeting. Sounds came from the front area. Familiar sounds and smells. The groan of a chair bearing a heavy weight. Rustle of papers. The smell of stale cigarette smoke. He knew there had to be a dispatcher and someone monitoring the phones. *Is there anyone else up there? Have to chance it.*

He opened the door to his left as quietly as he could. If the hinges weren't oiled and let out a screech, he was dead. The door swung open quietly. He glanced around. Enough light from the side parking lot came through the blind slats for him to see. *I'm in luck. The records room.* He checked the drawer labels until he found MISSING PERSONS, picked the file drawer lock, and gently pulled the drawer open. Jackson flipped a small penlight out of his pocket and, with deft fingers, rifled through the alphabetically captioned files and pulled out those of PERKINS, SANDRA and TALBOT, AMELIA. He noted the copier in the corner. He had to make copies of these reports and put them back in place but he could not do it here. He would have to take them to Godwin's. He slipped the files into his black windbreaker, retreated to the rear door, and left as quietly as he had entered.

In Charles Godwin's office, Jackson made two copies of each report, and copies of the photos in each file, then slipped them into his attaché case. He returned the police reports to the police headquarters' records room in the same manner in which he procured them. *They'll never know.*

Back at Charles Godwin's farm, Roger Jackson studied the reports, noted they were both made by the same officer, Detective Campbell, and studied the photos of tire tread tracks found at both scenes. To the trained eye it was obvious both tread tracks were identical. *Same vehicle. Confirms what I thought. Same guy.*

Charles Godwin and his wife, Joellyn, came into the office. Joellyn was carrying a tray with cups, sugar, cream, and a carafe of coffee. She set it down and dropped into a chair.

"Thought you'd be up to a cup of coffee, what with all your comings and goings."

"You read my mind."

"Charles said you were a heavy coffee drinker in Nam. Guess you haven't change."

Jackson saw the love, pride, and adoration in Godwin's eyes when he looked at his wife. Joellyn wasn't a beauty, but had a smile that lighted up a room and chased away gloom. Roger Jackson was happy for his Nam buddy. He smiled.

'What are you smiling about?" Godwin asked.

"Joellyn reminds me of my wife."

"Is she a happy wife like me?" Joellyn asked.

"I think so."

Godwin handed Roger Jackson an envelope. "This is a letter of introduction to the parents of the missing women. I happen to know them personally and I think they will cooperate and answer your questions. They will help you anyway they can."

"Thanks, Chuck."

Tomorrow, with his letter of introduction, he would visit the families.

* * * * *

Wednesday morning the rain beat down on the patio leaving puddles on everything; table, chairs, and grill. Laura sighed as she watched the wood line trees sway with the gusts. A synchronized ballet.

The house was clean-smelling after Lizzie's visit yesterday. There wasn't much for Laura to do. She dialed a number which was becoming familiar to her.

"Sue, this is Laura. How about I meet you at George's for lunch?"

"Great! Got some news to tell you."

"See you at noon."

* * * * *

George's held the same familiar faces. The "lunch bunch". Today, the restaurant smelled of wet umbrellas and rain coats. Laura shifted on the booth bench and waited for Sue Bader. The pretty vivacious blonde whirled into the restaurant grinning from ear to ear. She seemed oblivious to the dreary weather. She looked as if she would burst at the seams. Spying Laura in the booth, Sue hurried over.

"Laura, you ain't gonna believe this." She plunked down on the bench opposite Laura. "Pete asked me to marry him. I'm so thrilled and happy I could bust."

Laura reached over and covered Sue's hand. "I'm so happy for you, Sue. With that good news lunch is on me."

"No way, Jose. But thanks anyway."

The waitress took their orders and left.

Sue continued. "When he asked me I said, 'Did you have a change of heart?' and he said, 'No, but I got some unbelievable news'. He told me that he got a letter from a lawyer in Columbia saying that an anonymous benefactor left him some stocks and money. God bless that benefactor."

Laura drew in her breath. *Carleton Dinford*. Seeing the joy in Sue's eyes, and thinking of her father's wishes, tears welled in her own.

"Now don't get 'mushy' or you'll have me bust out in tears."

"Sorry, but I always cry when I'm happy."

The two women chatted through their lunch, Sue with her plans of marriage, and Laura telling her about Ryan and his foot. She did not mention Patrick's intended courtship, her stroll through the woods with Blarney, and the cigarette butts she found.

When Laura left George's she headed for Caper's to talk to her new friend, Caper Morgan.

Announced by the door chimes, Laura nodded to the sales clerk and proceeded to Caper's office and knocked.

"Come in."

Caper jumped up and hugged Laura. "Long time no see."

"I got involved with my neighbor and his injured foot."

"Ryan? What happened to him?"

Laura told Caper about Patrick's injury. Also about his intended courtship.

"I think that's great. I told you you'd make a striking couple."

"I don't know if it was in jest, or what."

"Ryan. Not on your life. He means every word. So, do you feel betrothed?"

"No, not really. Oh, Caper, I don't know. We haven't moved beyond the 'holding hands' stage. I feel like the gal that was left at the prom."

"Breathing space. And as you said, he's a bit laid up with his foot. Wait 'til he's up and about, my dear. You'll need track shoes to outrun him."

Laura laughed. "Maybe so. Just wanted you to be the first to know. And if it doesn't come off. C'est la vie!"

"I think I'll take a look at the new bridal gowns when I go "picking through" the garment district in New York next week."

A blush flushed Laura's face. "Don't be too hasty."

After another hug from Caper, Laura left.

* * * * *

He watched her walked back to her parked car and get in. The tension in his groin grew. *Love the way she swings her ass. Just askin' for it. Know there's got to be a great body under that rain coat. I'll find out pretty soon.* His vehicle moved around the town square.

A pick-up truck followed Laura's Mercedes out of town, west on 57, and turned off at the Hilltop Motel and headed back into Moultrie, as a dark blue rental crawled by.

* * * * *

"You did say your fiancée was Laura Crowder, didn't you?"

Patrick frowned. "Yes, Roger, why?"

"I think she's being stalked," then Roger Jackson hung up.

Patrick Ryan fell back into the cushions. The blood pounded in his brain. *By whom*? Then rethinking the cigarette butts found in the clearing behind Laura's home, he became both frightened and angry. He pushed himself up and called Robert.

"I've got to get up and moving, Robert."

"But Dr. Lyon said not to rush it."

"I have to. I just got news that Laura may be in some danger."

"Miz Crowder?" came the startled reply.

"Yes. Roger just called me and said she was being stalked."

"Lord Jesus," Robert uttered. "What can we do about it, Mr. Pat?"

"I don't know. I have to give it some thought."

* * * * *

"Ryan, I'll have to strap it real well if you intend to get up and move around," Dr Lyon blasted. "Told you not to rush it."

"Yes, I know, but things have changed. I have to get up and out."

"I don't imagine it will be too bad. A few torn ligaments. They seem to be mending pretty well. You'll just have to take the pain pills I gave you if you insist on walking."

"I will."

"Okay. But no running."

Patrick Ryan sighed. "I hope I don't have to."

* * * * *

Laura shook out her rain coat and hung it in the kitchen to dry. She wondered how Patrick was doing. "I'll give him a call."

"Laura, I'm glad you called. I'd like to come over this evening."

"Patrick, I thought you couldn't be up and about just yet."

"I just saw Dr. Lyon again. He said that I could walk about but not to run."

Laura thought of what Caper said. Track shoes. She wouldn't need them. He can't run just yet.

"Would you like me to fix dinner?"

"No, that won't be necessary. Mrs. Taylor has already started dinner. Are you planning to eat in or go out?"

It was a strange question coming from Patrick Ryan.

"I'm going to eat here. Why do you ask, Patrick?"

He didn't want to alarm her. "I'll be there by 8:00, and I'll bring a bottle of Frangelico," then he hung up.

* * * * *

He was prompt, arrived at 8:00, but unsteady on his feet. He handed the bottle of liqueur to Laura.

"Take it before I drop it."

"I think you're pushing it, Ryan. Should give yourself a little more time." She saw his eyes take in the hallway and the stairs.

Ryan checked the wall next to the door. "You don't have an alarm system, do you?"

"I don't think my parents had one installed. Why do you ask?"

"Just curious."

"No you're not, you had a reason to ask. What is it?"

"How about I sit down before you start the interrogation."

"I'm sorry. Let me help you. Lean..."

"Yeah, I know. Lean on me."

Patrick sat on the couch in the living room stretched out his long legs but did not cross his ankles. He wore a pair of tan pants and an easy pull-over knit shirt. He looked fairly comfortable to Laura.

"Need a pillow, or something?"

"I'll take the 'or something'."

Calling his bluff, she said, "Like what?"

"Frangelico."

Laura took the bottle into the kitchen, opened it and poured some into two small snifter glasses. Since he chose to dress casual, she was glad she wore a loose-fitting knit sweat suit. When she returned to the living room there was a small package on the coffee table. A very small one. She handed one glass to Patrick, set hers down, and said, "What's this?"

"It's for you."

Laura's hand shook as she reached for the tiny parcel. *Could it possibly be?* She untied the satin ribbon, opened the jewelry case and stared at the biggest pear-shaped diamond she ever saw. She did not realize her mouth was agape.

Ryan laughed. "Close your mouth."

"But, but, but..."

"I told you I'm courting you. This makes it official." He took the ring out of the case and said, "I hope it fits," and slipped it on Laura's ring finger.

It did, perfectly. Laura was still speechless.

"You know I have a jewelry store in Moultrie. I just called Sylvia Jacobs. She described what was in her inventory. I chose this and she delivered it. If you don't like it I can replace it with whatever you want"

"No, no! This is beautiful." She lifted her eyes and stared into Patrick's steely gray eyes. She seemed to read hope, love and desire in them and she felt as if a flight of butterflies burst in the pit of her stomach. "I thought you were jesting."

"I never jest, Laura. I mean every word I say." He took her hand back in his and raised it to his lips and kissed it. "I want you to marry me."

"Oh, Patrick, for someone that has only kissed me twice, no three times, are you sure?"

"I am, are you?"

The question drew her back, then she leaned forward and said, "Are you sure you're not marrying me so you can get my property and save yourself a million dollars?"

"That thought did cross my mind."

"Well, at least you're honest. Would you mind if I asked you to hold me?"

"Come into my arms and let me kiss you. A real engagement kiss."

Laura moved closer to him, lay forward and his arm went about her shoulders, gave a slight twist turning her face-up, and she found her back laying across his thighs. He took a sofa pillow and lifting her head, stuffed it under, which brought her face much closer to his. He brought his lips down on hers.

The surge of passion filled her body with tormenting heat. She drew up her knees onto the couch and turned her body partially toward Patrick. Her arms went about his neck and her fingers worked through his thick hair. She felt his lips open and she complied. Hot desire filled her. His kiss was maddening. She squirmed in her desire. All her resistance fled. She wanted more. Her lips and tongue fully responded to his. She felt his hand cover her breast. Gently, it explored its shape. Beneath her she felt his passion build into an erection. The hardness was tantalizing. She heard him softly groan.

Laura," he whispered, "I've got to stop this before I forget I'm handicapped and make love to you right here on the couch."

"Yes, Patrick, make love to me." She released a soft sigh. "Please make love to me."

The words were no more out of her mouth when his hand went under the knit sweat suit top and pulled her bra up over her breasts to somewhere around her neck. Softly, he squeezed the mounds. The nipples were puckered and he tweaked each one. Laura could only lie back and permit him anything.

"Laura, take off your clothes."

She raised up, removed her clothes and underwear, and turned her body toward Ryan. His hands caressed every inch, touched the small strawberry birthmark just below her navel, and slowly moved between her legs. His fingers taunted her small nub. Her breathing became ragged, and she squirmed under his finger pressure.

"Patrick, Patrick I'm, I'm..."

"Yes, my darling, you are."

With those words, Laura's orgasm burst with throbbing joy. She gave a gasping cry and wilted with sheer satisfaction.

Patrick moved her and got to his feet, undid his trousers, pushed them down to his knees, and released his erection so it could extend uninhibited. He pushed one leg between Laura's, then brought in the other. He slid down and took a nipple of her breast in his mouth and sucked. He heard her catch her breath. His own passion was under tight control. He released her nipple, moved upward, and guided his erected manhood into her tight, moist opening. Slowly he moved in and out of the sweet spot of womanhood, watching her face register passion and delight. With one hand on her breast and his mouth over hers, kissing and sucking, he plied the natural course of male supremacy.

Laura reveled in his entry and the movements of his desire. She was completely his. He could do anything and she would permit it. She lifted her hips to meet his, pushing harder with each thrust. Again, her arousal burned through her body, trailing all the way down to meet his erection. She wanted to buck and toss like a young colt. She opened her eyes and saw his hot passionate gaze meeting hers. Her fingers splayed over his back. She felt the wave of her orgasm start to rise, to crest, then to tumble and roll through her. She opened her mouth and released another deep groan of satisfaction. Patrick threw his head back and gave a primal growl, true to all sexual culminations, then lay spent on her body.

Laura's fingers combed his dark hair, pushing the errant lock back from his forehead. "Patrick, Patrick," was all she could whisper.

"Yes, my love. It was wonderful. Shall we try it again?"

"I don't know if I could make it a third time."

"Let me try. I want to make your body respond to mine. I'll be able to bring you to the heights again along with me." Patrick placed his lips on hers and they began the ritual of sexual bliss.

It was early Thursday morning, just before daylight, when Patrick Ryan left.

CHAPTER 13

Thursday noon, and Laura was still in bed. She lazily stretched and got up. Her thoughts were of Patrick. *His love-making was captivating. A third time. Even now I get all juiced up when I think of him in me. God, I do love the man and I can't explain how it happened. I want him in me right now. My God, what am I thinking?*

She held her hand out to admire her engagement ring. The beautiful pear-shaped diamond was breath-taking. *I'm going to be married. I can't believe it.*

She took a shower, put on her mother's terry robe and went downstairs to the kitchen. After zapping a leftover cup of coffee in the microwave she went out on the patio and raised her face toward the sun. The gentle gust of wind tugged at her robe, opening it to reveal her slim naked body. She didn't care. The cool breeze felt good on her bare skin, cooling her desire for Patrick. She sat on the patio chair, crossed her long legs, and sighed.

"What a beautiful day," she said aloud. "Clear and clean after the rain yesterday." She opened her robe further and enjoyed the sun's warm rays upon her bare skin. Her breast nipples were taunt, erect. Her thoughts swirled with Patrick. His hands upon her body, over her breasts, between her legs. He was everywhere on her. She gave a slight shiver thinking of all the passion spent last night.

She raised the cup to her lips just as a glint of reflected sunlight cut across the field behind her home. She quickly sat upright, closed her robe and squinted in the bright glare toward the clearing where she had found cigarette butts when she was walking Blarney. There was another flash, but the flash seemed to quickly jump up and down in a tempo, then stopped. Like someone sending Morse code.

Laura got up and went inside. *Could be the reflection of rain on a leaf twisting in the sunlight. But, leaves don't smoke.*

* * * * *

The afternoon mail brought responses from the insurance companies along with checks made out to her, as sole beneficiary, covering face value and dividend build-up on each policy. Substantial checks which had to be deposited immediately. She'd take them to the bank today and open a personal savings and checking account for herself.

Her wardrobe being limited she decided to get a few new things at Caper's and tell Caper the good news. She held up her left hand and sighed. The same thoughts ran through her mind. *Engaged to be married.* She shook her head. *I can't believe it.*

In the Moultrie Bank, Laura asked to see the accounts clerk, opened a savings account and deposited the full amounts of the checks, reserving ten thousand dollars for her checking account. The clerk quickly went and brought back the bank manager, who thanked Laura profusely for her patronage and advised her to put some of the insurance funds into CDs.

"You'll get a better interest rate."

The deposited money was then re-distributed to include a few short term CDs at a very good interest rate. The new checkbook was placed in her purse.

At Caper's, Laura chose a few casual outfits, another dinner dress, and accessories. She didn't realize she was humming.

"And why are you so happy on this Thursday afternoon?" Caper asked as she walked up to Laura and gave her a hug.

Laura held up her left hand and the solitaire diamond glistened

"My God! Can you lift your hand. I don't think I've ever seen a diamond that big. It's beautiful." She gave Laura another hug. "I'm so happy for you."

"I'm so happy for me, too. You were right, Caper, Patrick said he never jests. He meant every word."

"Told you. How about going to the club for lunch and you can tell me about any plans you may be thinking."

"Sounds good to me. I'll meet you there at 1:00."

Laura picked up her purchases and left.

* * * * *

Edmond led Laura to Caper Morgan's table. The two women ordered wine and sat back to await their order.

"You look like the Cheshire Cat, all grins."

"I can't tell you how happy I am, Caper. I would have never imagined, in a million years, that I would come down to Moultrie, South Carolina and in three short weeks become engaged to be married."

The wine arrived. They gave the waitress, Shirley, their lunch order, and settled back to enjoy the wine.

"How is Ryan's foot coming along?"

"He's managing very well."

Caper's eyebrows lifted and Laura felt the blush cover her face.

"Yes, I can see he has recuperated quite well." Caper said with a tight smile on her face.

To change the subject, Laura told Caper of her walk with Blarney and what she found in the clearing. Also, she mentioned the tire tracks on the other side of the stream.

"Do you think anyone is going there? But for what purpose?"

"Don't know. Patrick was worried about it. Come to think of it, that may be the reason he asked about an alarm system in my house."

"Do you have one?"

"No."

"Get a dog."

"'Get a dog', I can't be bothered with an animal, Caper. They're like children and need too much attention."

"Borrow Ryan's dog for a while. If anyone is 'casing' your house they might change their mind if they know you have a dog on the premises."

Laura thought about it for a few minutes. "Might be a good idea. Blarney is well trained. He knows me and obeys commands."

"Good! Speak to Ryan about it. I'm sure he will see it as a good idea."

Their chicken salad orders arrived and Shirley set the plates before them. "Will there be anything else, ladies?"

Both women shook their heads.

"This looks great. On second thought, I think I'll have another glass of Chardonnay, please," Laura said. "I'm celebrating."

Shirley smiled. "What's the occasion?"

"My engagement."

"Congratulations. Who's the lucky man?"

"Patrick Ryan."

A cloud seemed to pass over the waitress's face then quickly disappeared. She spun about and left.

Caper noticed the waitress's reaction, too. "Maybe she had a crush on Ryan."

"Could be," Laura said.

"Have you set a date as yet. I know it's too soon to ask, but..."

"No. I'm not in a hurry. Besides, it seems that if I'm going to stay here in Moultrie I've got a lot of business to take care of. There's moving all my stuff down from Richmond, applying for a license to practice in South Carolina, change of address, just so many things to do."

"I see. Well, don't let the burden get you down." She picked up her fork. "Let's enjoy our lunch."

While they were chatting, Shirley brought Laura's second glass of wine and set it next to her plate, nodded and left. Unbeknownst to Laura, Shirley had put a small amount of phenolphthalein in her glass of wine. She had used this white crystalline powder on other club members to get revenge for their groping hands or unwarranted complaints by women.

Laura deliberately avoided eye contact with Shirley.

When their lunch was over, the two women promised to get together soon, and left the clubhouse.

Laura climbed into her Mercedes and followed Caper's car out of the parking lot, east along Lakeside Drive, then they both turned left onto the county road that led north into Moultrie. Laura was surprised she was feeling a bit dizzy. *Maybe I shouldn't have had the second glass. Nah! A second glass never hurt me before.*

She gave a wave to Caper then turned left onto the county road that passed the Moultrie Correctional Unit. Her head was spinning, her driving became erratic, and she pulled over to the side of the road. She felt nauseous, turned up the air conditioning, and rested her head on the steering wheel.

A few minutes past when she heard the tapping on her driver's side window. Laura looked up and recognized the face of the deputy that helped her with her groceries. She lowered the window half way.

"Are you all right, Miz Crowder?" he asked.

"I was feeling a bit sick. Thought it best to pull over until it passed."

He glanced around. "Can I take you home. You can get the car later."

Laura thought of it, and shook her head." No, I'll be all right."

The deputy put his hand on the door handle and tried to open it but Laura had not released the door locks. She was about to do it then decided not to. "I'll be okay. Thank you for stopping." She put the car in gear and slowly pulled out onto the county road. In her rearview mirror she saw the police officer get into his car and follow. She was particularly careful to maintain proper speed and control. Out on Highway 57 she turned east toward Moultrie and then turned left into her driveway. She wondered if the officer would follow her into her driveway. He did not. She saw his patrol car pass and continue on toward Moultrie.

At home, she lay on the couch and rested. *Must have been something I ate.* She closed her eyes and the officer's face came to mind. She reviewed the happening. *Why did he try my door handle to open the door? Strange.* In a few minutes she drifted off to sleep.

The ringing of the phone awoke her.

"Hello."

"Laura, Patrick. I tried to reach you this morning and at noon but could not."

"Oh, Patrick, I went into Moultrie. I received some insurance checks in the mail and I had to deposit them right away. Had lunch at the club with Caper."

"You had me worried."

"Patrick, what did you say the name of the sheriff's deputy was?"

"Deputy Clark, Jimmy Clark. Why do you ask?"

"Coming from the club I got a bit nauseous and had to pull over to the side of the road. Officer Clark came to my window and wanted me to leave the car and he would drive me home. I almost did but changed my mind."

"How come he was so 'johnny-on-the-spot'?"

"I don't know." There was a long pause. "Are you there, Patrick?"

"Yes, my darling. I was just thinking." The hum of silence filled the phone. "Laura, I want you to come over this evening for dinner. Mrs. Taylor has promised a wonderful meal in celebration of our engagement."

"You told Robert and Mrs. Taylor."

"Yes, and they are as happy as 'two bugs in a rug'. I feel we should at least comply."

"Oh, yes, Patrick. I think it's very nice of Mrs. Taylor to want to fix a celebration meal for us."

"Make it about 7:00, my darling. I'll be waiting."

* * * * *

Selecting one of her new purchases, Laura donned a pair of bright red silk pants, a white silk peasant blouse, and added strings of red summer jewelry with matching earrings. She was anxious to see Patrick again.

"A new outfit?" Patrick asked. "You look stunning, as usual." He was standing by the bar supported by a cane. His attire was casual, but elegant. One errant coil of dark hair hung over his forehead.

"You look rather dashing yourself." She walked over to him and pressed her lips to his.

"Careful girl, or you'll release the beast in me."

They both chuckled.

Laura, visualizing the "beast" in him, felt a warm scattering of butterfly wings whirl in the pit of her stomach. She put her lips to his ear and whispered, "Perhaps later." His startled reaction was comical and she laughed aloud.

"Are you toying with me, you little vixen? Beware, or I might forego our celebration dinner and haul you up to my bed chamber."

Laura accepted the glass of Chardonnay from Patrick. She was giddy with happiness.

"Caper Morgan was quite happy with the news of our engagement. We celebrated at the club with lunch and wine. I mentioned to Shirley I was celebrating our engagement. She didn't seem too happy about it. I guess it was the second glass she brought that made me nauseous."

"Careful with Shirley. I have been watching her. I've had some complaints regarding after-effects. I think she puts something in the food or drink of those she's unhappy with. She might have put something in your second glass of wine to make you ill. I'm just waiting to catch her, and when I do, she's history."

Robert came in, a gleaming smile stretching his face, and placed a silver salver on the coffee table. In the center of the tray was a small vial holding a white cymbidium orchid. Two china plates, oyster forks, and linen cocktail napkins lay on the tray. Small hors d'oeuvres of butterflied shrimp stuffed with crab meat, and tiny cheese balls wrapped in *prosciutto* accompanied with herb crackers completed the lovely presentation.

Laura clapped her hands and emitted an audible "Ahhh."

Robert said, "May I offer my congratulations, Miz Crowder, or may I call you Miz Laura, now that you'll be family."

"Yes to both, Robert, and thank you and Mrs. Taylor for this lovely tray of goodies."

"As they say 'you ain't seen nuttin' yet'." He turned and left the room.

Patrick, smiling, hobbled over to the couch and sat.

Laura fixed a plate and handed it to him, then one for herself, and sat down on the couch close beside him.

"Patrick, I've been thinking. Since, obviously, I'm going to live here in Moultrie, there's a huge amount of details I have to take care of, such as moving my possessions down here, applying for a license to practice in South Carolina, changing my address."

"Yes, darling, I know, and I can be of help to you."

"How's that?"

"Well, I can take care of the moving part. I'll contact a moving company in Richmond, have them pack up your belongings and ship them here."

"That will be a terrible expense, packing everything, and all."

Ryan raised his brows and looked at Laura. "Really, Laura, it will be less wear and tear on everybody. It's the simple solution. As for the change of address, we can do that all by computer, upstairs. Even applying for your license to practice, that, too, can be done on the computer."

Laura sat back in amazement. "I never gave it a thought but if it can work that way it would be wonderful."

"It can."

She picked up a stuffed shrimp and popped it into her mouth. "Delicious!"

Ryan did the same. "Yes, Mrs. Taylor outdid herself."

While they nibbled on the hors d'oeuvres, Laura mentioned about the glinting from the woods line, and what Caper said about getting a dog.

"Do you think someone is watching my house in hopes of robbing it?"

"No, I don't. News of your parents' death spread like wildfire through Moultrie. If they were going to rob the house they would have done so before you got here. As for getting a dog, we'll have to work something out for Blarney to spend the nights at your house."

"You seem to have taken care of my problems in one fell swoop."

He lifted her hand to his lips and kissed it. "That's what I'm here for, Laura. I will forever rid you of your problems because your problems become mine."

"Dinner will be served, Mr. Pat, Miz Laura," Robert announced from the doorway.

Ryan struggled to his feet and took his cane. "Shall we see what Mrs. Taylor has fixed for our engagement dinner?"

"Oh, yes, Patrick. I know it will be wonderful."

And wonderful it was.

Under the crystal chandelier, in the center of the table, was a silver punch bowl filled with potted white cymbidium orchids surrounded with sorghum grass. The table was set with beautiful silver-rimmed china plates, sterling flatware, and crystal glasses rimmed in silver. The dinner, served by Robert, was a crisp salad, Beef Wellington, rare, pencil-thin asparagus with Hollandaise sauce, baby carrots with Mandarin oranges in a sugar and wine sauce, and tiny fresh baked Parker House rolls. It was a tableau of decadence.

Laura sighed as Robert held her chair. "I hope it all meets with your expectations, Miz Laura."

"Indeed, indeed! Robert. A feast for the Gods."

Robert's smile lit his face. "I'll be sure to tell Miz Taylor that."

Laura, feeling very relaxed, smiled at Patrick. "I don't know why you don't weigh 300 pounds. With a cook like Mrs. Taylor, I'll gain weight."

"We don't eat this way every night, Laura. Generally, Mrs. Taylor serves very balanced meals. She's very health-conscious."

"That's very good news for me."

* * * * *

Laura gave a groan as she sat next to Ryan on the couch.

"What a wonderful engagement dinner, Patrick. I thank you very much."

"My pleasure. I am sure Mrs. Taylor is jumping for joy that she pleased you."

"How could she not. It was sumptuous."

Robert appeared at the doorway. "Mr. Pat, if there's nothin' else, I'll retire."

"I won't need anything else, Robert. Go ahead upstairs."

When they were alone, Laura felt her stomach stir. This time it wasn't from something she ate. She was anticipating Patrick's love-making.

Ryan turned to her. "Laura, will you stay the night with me?"

"Yes, Patrick, but I didn't bring a nightgown."

"My love, you won't need one."

Together they walked to the elevator and got off at the second floor.

* * * * *

While Laura and Patrick were making steamy love, a lock pick was being inserted into the front door lock at Laura's home. The man casually flipped on the lights, walked through the foyer, glanced about and admired the interior, then took the stairs two at a time.

On the second floor landing he poked his head into the bedrooms and finally chose the one Laura used.

This is her room. I can smell her.

He walked to the bathroom and touched the terry cloth robe she wore on the patio. He lifted it from the hook, smelled it and felt his erection build. He remembered her body as he watched her, with binoculars, open the robe and reveal herself to him. She was beautiful. He had jerked off then and was ready to do so now. *No, not now.* He pushed his erection down, threw the robe over the tub rim, and then turned to see what was in the bureau drawers.

He sifted through Laura's lingerie, lifted a pair of panties to his nose and sniffed. Her cologne permeated her personal clothing. He swallowed the build-up of drool. *I could lick her cunt.*

He took the panties with him as he chose a spot to settle down and wait for his prey to return. Anticipation dwindled, and at 3:00 a.m. he got up, went downstairs into the den and took a piece of paper from the desk pad.

He wrote: **I WAS HERE**.

* * * * *

A bit shy, and wrapped in one of Patrick's robes, Laura went into the breakfast room where Robert had set the table for breakfast. She wondered what he and Mrs. Taylor would think of her staying overnight. She walked to the credenza and from the carafe poured herself a cup of fresh brewed coffee. Glancing out the window she saw Robert walking with Blarney behind Patrick's home. He was headed for the house.

A few minutes later she was joined by Patrick. He moved to her side and wrapped his arms about her.

"Have I told you today that I love you?"

She wrapped her arms about his neck and nuzzled into the curve of his chin. "I love you, too, Patrick." She pushed away. "What do you think Robert and Mrs. Taylor will think about my staying the night?"

"Not to worry. I told them that I was worried about you being over there alone and wanted you to be here, with me, in the guest room."

"But I didn't sleep in the guest room."

"They'll never know. I went in there and messed up the bedding to make it look like you slept in there."

Laura planted a kiss on his lips. "Thank you, darling, for protecting my reputation."

They both laughed.

Robert appeared, carrying a tray of eggs, bacon, sliced ham, corn muffins, jams, and toast.

"Know y'all can't be too hungry after last night's dinner, but Miz Taylor said something about keeping up your stamina."

Laura felt the flush fill her face and she turned away from Robert.

"We will try to do just that," Patrick said with a snicker.

* * * * *

Laura walked into her home and went upstairs to change. She had showered at Patrick's, but wanted to get out of last night's clothes.

On the boudoir chair was a pair of her panties. She picked them up and frowned. *I didn't leave these here. How did they get here?* She put them back into the bureau drawer and went into the bathroom. Her robe was flung over the tub rim. Fear clutched her throat. *Someone's been in here.*

She went to the phone and dialed Patrick.

"Patrick..."

He recognized the fear in her voice. "What's wrong, Laura?"

"Someone has been in the house last night."

"I'll be over in a few minutes."

* * * * *

Patrick, using his cane, hobbled into the foyer, went on into the living room, and settled on the couch.

"How do you know, Laura?"

"A pair of my panties were thrown on the chair in my bedroom and my robe was tossed over the tub rim in the bathroom."

"You didn't leave them there yourself?"

"No, definitely not. And when I went to call you I found this note next to the phone."

Patrick got up. "I'm going in and call Sheriff Mellichampe."

Laura went with him and stood by his side as he spoke with the sheriff.

"He'll be here in a few minutes. Make a pot of coffee, Laura. The sheriff would probably enjoy a cup. As to your not being here, in the house last night, just say you were not feeling well so I suggested you spend the night. It's plausible, but no doubt he'll see it for what it is."

Laura went into the kitchen, took out a percolator and made a full pot of coffee, placed mugs, sugar and cream on the kitchen table and returned to the living room. Patrick was white as a sheet.

"Are you all right, Patrick?"

"Yes. I was just thinking how close that was. If you hadn't spent the night..." his voice drifted off.

"Yes, I get a sick feeling in my stomach when I think of it."

The door chimes rang and Laura admitted a tall, barrell-chested man in full uniform.

"Miss Crowder, I'm Sheriff Mellichampe." He extended his hand.

Laura accepted it and led him into the living room.

Patrick got to his feet and shook hands with the officer.

"Mr. Ryan, good to see you. Now tell me what this is all about."

149

Laura brought the coffee pot from the kitchen and poured three cups and handed one to the sheriff. Then she told him of what she found when she came in this morning and showed him the note. The sheriff took the note by the corner, placed it in a plastic envelope and slipped into his inside coat pocket..

"You were not in the house last night?"

"No. I was over at Mr. Ryan's. We had dinner and I, er, was not feeling too well so Mr. Ryan invited me to spend the night." She could feel the heat on her face, but it seems Sheriff Mellichampe did not notice.

"Good thing you weren't. Situation would be entirely different if you had." He continued, "Have you found anything else missing? Jewelry? Silverware?"

"No, nothing."

"Then it seems you were the purpose of the break-in."

Laura felt a shiver slide down her back. "Why?" she managed to say through clenched teeth.

"That I'll find out," the sheriff said.

Laura softly said, "Maybe that's why there were cigarette butts and tire tracks down in the woods behind my house. The person must have been "casing" the house." She explained to the sheriff how she had come to find these and noticed his eyes squint in thought.

The big man stood, drained his cup and said, "Good coffee. Thank you. I'll be in touch." He turned toward Patrick and nodded. "Mr. Ryan, take care of that foot," and let himself out of the house.

"Isn't much to go on," Patrick said, "but he's very efficient. He might be able to get a print from the note."

"It's a bit unsettling to find myself in the victim's place instead of the lawyer's." She sagged back into the couch pillows.

Ryan took her hand and rolled it gently in his. "Laura, I think I'll bring Blarney over to spend the nights here with you. Robert can pick him up in the morning, if that's all right with you."

"Yes, oh yes. He'll be a great comfort to me."

"Good!" Ryan got up and went to the front door. Laura walked beside him. He turned and put his arm about her. "If anything ever happened to you..." his voice trailed off. He pulled her to him and pressed a possessive kiss upon her lips.

She fully responded and clung to him, her hand trailing down his arm as he turned and left..

* * * * *

Laura went back into the den, dialed Sue at work and asked to meet her at George's.

"I'll be there. I have some more good news."

When Laura entered George's Sue Bader was waiting. She waved her hand to get Laura's attention, and the two women hugged each other.

Sue held out her hand and Laura saw the diamond solitaire. "Pete and I have set a date for our wedding. June 4th. I'm so happy I could bust."

Laura took Sue's hand. "I'm so happy for you, Sue."

They gave their order to the waitress and sat back.

"I was so excited about my good news I didn't ask why you wanted to meet. You look a bit tired or strained. You okay?"

Laura looked about, leaned over and softly said. "Last night, at Patrick's, Mrs. Taylor, his cook, fixed a wonderful dinner in celebration of our engagement." She held out her hand and Sue's eyes widened is surprise.

"Engaged?" She took Laura's hand and studied the pear-shaped diamond ring. "Lordy, that's the biggest diamond solitaire I've ever seen."

"Size doesn't matter. It's what it means that counts," Laura said. "Anyway, after dinner I stayed at Patrick's house." She saw Sue smile and quickly added, "In the guest bedroom."

"Sure, sure, I know, for appearances sake. Go on."

"Well, while I was at Patrick's, someone broke into my house, went upstairs and looked through my belongings, and left a note."

"What did the note say?"

"I WAS HERE." Laura glanced about. "Patrick called the sheriff, he came, took the note and said that since nothing was taken, it appears that someone was after me."

Sue's face registered horror. "Oh, no. Oh, Laura, could it be the same maniac that took Amelia Talbot and Sandra Perkins?"

"I hope not." Laura told Sue about what she found in the woods when she walked Blarney. Cigarette butts, tire tracks, and crushed grass where someone had stood in the woods directly behind her house. "Patrick said no one is supposed to be in those woods. Private property. Sheriff Mellichampe said the same thing."

"Had to be the same guy. He must be psycho to be handling your panties and robe. Do you have an alarm system in the house?"

"No, but Patrick is going to have Blarney spend the nights with me. Don't know how much protection he will be but it will be a comfort to have him close by."

Their orders were brought and they both ate quietly. Thoughts of fear ran through Laura's mind.

"I know I have a lot of planning to do for my wedding, but if you need me for anything please call me. I'll be there for you."

Laura put her hand over Sue's. "You're a good friend, Sue. I'll keep that in mind."

CHAPTER 14

Roger Jackson sat in Charles Godwin's home office and studied the notes he had taken when he visited the parents of Amelia Talbot and Sandra Perkins. Neither woman had been married. Talbot, a school teacher, and Perkins, a bank teller. Somewhere he thought, there had to be a connection with these women and their abductor.

Where are they? If I had taken them, molested them, then killed them, where would I dump the bodies?

Godwin entered the office. "How are things going, Dodge?"

The name was a carry-over from the Nam days. Roger-Dodger. Jackson shook his head. "Let me pose a question to you, Chuck. If you killed a woman here in Moultrie County, where would you dispose of the body?"

"Whoa! I haven't given any thought about killings these days. Anyway, I guess if I did want to get rid of a body I would take it to the lake."

Jackson studied the handsome black man. "Yeah, I thought that would be the likely place, but bodies eventually float. Has any bodies been discovered lately?"

"No." Godwin scratched his head. "Maybe they were shackled in cement, like in the old gangster movies."

"Think I'll go down to the lake pier and ask around."

"Come have some breakfast first. Joellyn's been cooking up a storm. Bacon, eggs, grits, biscuits with milk gravy."

"Say no more. I'm coming."

Roger settled into the kitchen chair and helped himself to huge servings. He glanced at Joellyn who was munching on salted soda crackers. Jackson smiled.

* * * * *

The sun was hot. The month of May had just begun. Jackson walked out on the pier where several men were fishing.

"Hi, guys, catching anything?"

One old codger, flannel shirt open revealing a stained undershirt, looked up at Jackson. "Nary a one, today, but I keeps tryin'."

"What kind of fish would you catch here? Catfish?"

"Nah, bream if ya lucky. Catfish I hunts at night."

"At night?"

The old man, feeling important from the attention he was getting, set his rod down, lit a cigarette, and stared at Roger Jackson. "Boy, you don't knows much about fishin', do ya?"

The word "boy" brought Jackson's hard stare on the old geezer. "Haven't heard the word "boy" in a long time."

The old man snickered. "All us old guys are called 'good ol' boys' so's you don't have to take unkindly to the word, mister."

"Sorry." Jackson moved closer to the old man. "Tell me how you hunt catfish at night?"

"Well," he drawled, "I gets in my boat. I wear my miner's hat, it has a lamp on it. I cruise along the banks of the feeders," seeing the question on the black man's face, added, "feeders are the little streams that come into this here lake." Jackson nodded, and the man continued. "I drags my hands under the lip of the bank feeling for the pockets where the catfish are sleeping and when I feel one I grab it."

"Are you kidding me?"

"Hell, no! You can pet the damn things right in their beds. I plug my fingers into the gill and pull the damn thing aboard."

"What about snakes?"

"Nah! The only thing you gotta watch out for is the snappin' turtles. Could lose a couple of fingers if they grabs ya."

"Have you been night fishing lately?"

"Goes every night I can. Have a system. One night I start at a certain point, then the next night I pick up from there and I continues." The old codger saw the doubt in Jackson's eyes and said, "If you wants I can take you out some night."

Jackson thought of mosquitoes, and other insects and shook his head. "Thank you, but I don't think I have the patience to be a fisherman."

"You're right about that. Sometimes I'm sittin' out there for lots o' hours and catch nary a one."

"Thanks, old timer. I appreciate you taking the time to tell me about night catfish-ing."

"Where are ya staying, boy?"

This time the term rolled off Jackson's shoulders, "With Charles Godwin."

"Oh, yeah, I knows him. He's another one of the 'good ol' boys. Tell him Zeke Mills sends his best."

"I'll do that."

* * * * *

Jackson drove north to the town of Moultrie and entered George's Sandwich Shop. His eyes immediately caught Laura as she sat with another young woman, having lunch. He noted that the conversation between them appeared somewhat strained. The two women were frowning. He quickly glanced about the room to see if they were the center of attention to anyone else. They were not, so he ordered his lunch and watched them. When they got up to leave he dropped several bills on the table and went out behind them. The blonde crossed the street and entered the county administration building. Laura Crowder headed down the street and entered Caper's.

Being Friday afternoon, business began to pick up. Quite a few cars were parked around the square. He parked his rental, turned off the engine and waited.

* * * * *

Laura entered Caper's shop.

"Caper, I have to tell you what happened at my place last night." Laura went into a long account of the break-in, the sheriff coming out to the house, and what was said. "It gives me the creeps that someone went through my things."

Caper leaned over and hugged Laura. "You've got to be careful. If the sheriff thinks the intruder is after you, you have to be very careful. Perhaps having the dog with you will make a difference."

They spoke for a few more minutes then Laura got up and left.

Outside, Laura walked to her car, got in, started it and headed out of town for her home.

Behind her, but not too close, was a pick-up truck. The driver was slouched down behind the wheel. He followed, as he did previously, then turned around at the Hilltop Motel. He paid no attention to the dark blue rental car that trailed behind his, and continued on when he made his turn.

The dark blue rental turned into the driveway to ERIN, stopped in front of the house and the tall black man got out and rang the bell.

"Mr. Jackson. So good to see you again, sir." enthused Robert. "Come in, come in."

"Mr. Ryan about?"

"Yes, sir, he's in the living room."

The investigator knew the way, went in and saw Ryan sitting where he last saw him. "I have some news for you, and a license plate number. I can call New York and have it traced from there but I thought you would like to know."

Patrick Ryan hobbled to the bar, poured a stiff shot of bourbon with a splash of water and handed it to Jackson. He poured himself of glass of scotch and went back and sat down.

"Tell me what you know."

"Your woman, Laura Crowder, was followed again by the same man. Don't know what his intentions are, but it seems odd for him to follow her twice. Stalking."

Ryan then told Jackson of last night's intruder into Laura's house, and what she found in the woods when walking Blarney.

"Sheriff thinks this person is after Laura."

"Sounds like he is. Nothing taken, just fiddling with her underwear and robe. Sounds like a psycho."

"Scares the hell out of me."

"How's the foot?"

"Much better, but I still can't run. However, I'm managing very well."

"Good." Jackson swallowed his drink, turned and left the room, saying over his shoulder, "I'll be seeing you."

* * * * *

Fred Tanner drove back to the county district garage in his pick-up truck, and sat down next to a school bus. A fellow worker came up to him and asked why he looked so troubled.

"It's a personal matter, Ed. I have to work it out in my own mind."

Ed walked away.

That evening, Fred waited for Cheryl to put Tommy to bed then asked her to sit down, he had something he wanted to ask with her.

"Honey, if you overheard a conversation that was troubling to you, would you tell someone else?"

"Depends. Is it a life or death conversation?"

"Could be. I'll have to give it some more thought before I do anything about it."

Cheryl Tanner frowned. It wasn't like her husband to be so elusive, but she knew that sooner or later he would tell her. She shook her head, went over to him and lightly touched the scar on his cheek.

"Looks like it's healing nicely. How did you say you got it?"

"At one of our training meetings. Hose nozzle hit me on the side of my face. Hurt like hell." He rubbed his hand over the healing scar.

* * * * *

Zeke Mills slowly dragged his hand under the ledge of the bank on Indian Creek, searching for a pocket where he expected a catfish to be hole-up. His hand touched the smooth skin of his prize. It felt long and of good size. He slid his hand under the smooth skin and slowly lifted it to the surface, hoping to snag the gill with his other hand. His terrified scream rang through the darkness of the woods. The light from his miner's hat revealed a person's white arm.

* * * * *

Sheriff Mellichampe parked his patrol car in front of Zeke Mills's river cottage and got out. Zeke was on the porch pacing back and forth. He grabbed the sheriff's arm and led him down to the creek.

"Never had sech a thing happen afore. I's scared to death." He shivered."I touched it."

"Settle down, Zeke, and show me what you found."

They walked to the boat, and Zeke Mills told the sheriff to get in.

"Where are we going?"

"Out on the creek. I'll show ya."

Zeke Mills paddled directly to the spot.

"I don't want to do it ag'in. You do it, sheriff."

"What do you want me to do?"

"Reach under the bank there and pull up what you feel."

Mellichampe looked doubtful. "You crazy. I might get snake-bit."

"No ya wont. Jes do it."

Sheriff took off his light Eisenhower jacket, rolled up his sleeve, and reached under the embankment. At first he felt nothing, then his hand touched smooth skin. He took hold of it and raised it to the surface. It was a right arm. On the pinkie was a small ring.

Mellichampe's eyes widened as he stared at the ring. He recognized it. The revealed part of human body belonged to Sandra Perkins, the bank teller. He stared at the arm for a minute or two, then slowly lowered it back into the water. He took out his handkerchief, tore it and tied it to a branch just above.

"Get me back to your place, Zeke."

He hurried to his patrol car and phoned in to headquarters.

"Mellichampe here. Need the Search and Recovery Dive Team out here on Indian Creek, left bank, below Zeke Mills's place. Marked the place with my handkerchief. Think we found one of our missing women."

All the baby and police scanners within receiving range garbled out the sheriff's conversation. Because of the early morning hour, no person heard it, except one.

* * * * *

The dive team found the body of Sandra Perkins under the ledge of the creek bank. They moved down stream and discovered the body of Amelia Talbot wedged in the same manner. By order of the coroner, Dr. Lyon, the bodies were transported to Columbia to the State Medical Examiner and Coroner's Lab.

News travels fast in a small town, especially on a Saturday morning when it seems everybody in the county is in town. Roger Jackson heard the news and decided to inform the sheriff of his presence and what he had observed, which he did, omitting his burglary of the missing persons investigation papers.

"Knew Ryan would contact an investigator from out-of-state. Kind of thought someone was somewhere in town. Nice to meet you, Mr. Jackson." He reached out and shook the big black's hand. "From what you told me, you have a very impressive background in police work. I may use you as we go into this murder if it's okay with you."

"Okay with me," Jackson replied.

"Why don't you hang around for awhile?"

"I'll do that."

The sheriff took the license plate number Jackson copied and sent it through to Columbia. The name returned was Fred Tanner.

"I'll send Clark out there to pick him up for questioning."

* * * * *

Officer Jim Clark walked up to the front door of Tanner's home, rang the bell. Fred opened the door.

"Sheriff wants you to come to headquarters to answer a few questions."

"What for?"

"Ain't for me to say, Tanner. Get your jacket and let's go."

"I can't leave here. The baby is sleeping. Cheryl is at work."

"Ask a neighbor to baby-sit."

"What's this all about?"

"Can't say. Call someone."

Fred Tanner went to the phone and called his mother-in-law."

At police headquarters, Sheriff Mellichampe led Fred Tanner into the interrogation room and told him to sit.

"Mr. Tanner, where were you on the night of April 3rd of this month?"

"April 3rd? I don't know. What day of the week was it?"

"Friday. It was the day Amelia Talbot disappeared."

"Why are you asking me about Amelia Talbot. I hardly know her."

"Well, you work for the district garage, where the school buses are maintained and housed. Talbot occasionally drove a school bus. You must have met her."

"Yes, I know Amelia. I've talked to her several times. A lovely person."

"We have reason to believe she's not missing, but murdered."

Fred Tanner jumped up from his chair. "You don't think I would kill Amelia, do you?"

The sheriff looked down at the sheet of paper he was holding. "Can you tell me where you were on the April 3rd?"

Tanner's face was ashen. "I'd have to look at my home calendar, but if it was a Friday, I could've been at the firehouse."

"What would you have been doing at the firehouse?"

"Maintenance and equipment instruction. Possibly cleaning equipment. Had a meeting just last week, the 17th."

"That was the night Sandra Perkins, the bank teller, disappeared. We now know she was murdered."

Tanner dropped back into the chair, dumbstruck.

There was a disturbance outside. Deputy Clark opened the door and stuck his head into the room. "Sheriff, Mz Tanner is here. She's mighty upset. Raisin' Cain."

"I'll be right there." The big man stood.

Tanner jumped up again.

"Not you, Tanner. You're not going anywhere right now."

Fred Tanner sank down, as if in quicksand, and stared at the officer in disbelief. "I didn't do anything. Why are you holding me?"

"Just sit here. I'll be right back." The officer left the room.

Outside, the loud quarreling subsided. Tanner could hear the front door slam. Soon, Sheriff Mellichampe returned.

"Your wife is going to shut her shop and go home to wait for you."

Once more Tanner made a move to get up and the sheriff put his hand on Tanner's shoulder, holding him down.

"Tell me, Tanner, why were you following Laura Crowder's car. Twice."

Tanner's face drained completely. He looked like a dead man. He spun his head and looked in all directions. Especially at the mirror. Then he leaned forward toward the sheriff and softly asked, "Is there anyone on the other side of that mirror?"

Sheriff turned to look at the mirror. "Shouldn't be."

"Can you check?"

"Why?"

"'Cause I'm going to say something that could cost me my life."

Mellichampe got up, went out and closed the door. In a minute he was back and shook his head. "No one in there."

"The reason I was following Crowder's car was because I overheard Deputy Clark say some very suggestive things about her, saying he was fucking her. Even said she had a red birth mark below her belly button."

Mellichampe's bushy eyebrows rose. "What's that got to do with your following her car?"

"I saw him follow her car a couple of times. I followed to protect her. I know that woman wouldn't have anything to do with the likes of Clark. She's too refined, too educated. I don't know if what he said about the birth mark is true, but Clark is hot for her."

Mellichampe recalled what happened at Laura Crowder's house. What she said about her findings in the woods. Cigarette butts, tire marks, the sharp glint that came from the woods line. He got up. Tanner remained seated.

"Do you smoke?"

Tanner frowned. "No, I don't."

"Tanner, I'm going to keep you here in lock-up until I can check out some things. I'm not charging you with anything but, for appearances sake, I need you to stay in the jail. Do you understand?"

Fred Tanner looked into the officer's face for his answer. "I think I do."

Sheriff Tanner called Officer Clark and told him to lock up Tanner.

Clark nodded. "With pleasure."

* * * * *

"I'm sorry, but I have to ask. Do you have a red birth mark below your navel?"

Laura sputtered in disbelief. How in the hell does he know that?

Patrick jumped up as quickly as he could.

"I think you're over-stepping your bounds, sheriff."

"No. I need the verification. It may give me the name of our killer."

Laura shook her head as if to clear it. "The killer?"

"Let me explain..."

And Sheriff Mellichampe told Patrick and Laura the entire scenario, starting with Zeke Mills's discovery, talking to Roger Jackson, apprehending Fred Tanner, but he left out the name given by Tanner.

"...so I'd like you to do me a favor. I'm going back to the office, pick up our man that does the photography, and drive to the back of your property. If I remember correctly, there's an old logging road that comes into the back of this place. I'll call you and what I want you to do is go out on your patio, stand there for a few minutes, then go back into the house. Will you do that for me, Miss Crowder?"

Of course, sheriff."

* * * * *

"Make sure you get a good picture of those tire tracks, Billy. I'm going to cross the stream and walk a bit further."

Mellichampe walked back to his car and made the call to Laura then he crossed the stream and saw that he had a very good view of the back of the Crowder house. He noticed the cigarette butts and trampled grass. He pulled up his binoculars and peered through them. They brought Laura's face up close as she stepped out onto the patio. Then, much to his surprise, she did an unusual thing. She opened the fly of her pants, lifted her knit shirt, and exposed her birth mark. He could see it clearly with the binoculars. Then she quickly re-fixed her clothes and went into the house.

Sheriff Mellichampe smiled. *She's got guts.*

* * * * *

Jackson shifted in the swivel armchair causing the chair to creak.

"How come sheriff wants you here?" asked Deputy Clark.

"I didn't ask."

"You from Columbia? SLED?"

"'SLED', what's that?"

"South Carolina State Law Enforcement Division."

"No."

Clark leaned back in his chair and lit a cigarette.

"Those things will kill you," Roger Jackson said.

"Yeah. Something will."

The officer manning the switchboard, mashed out his cigarette and picked up the ringing phone, cutting off the nerve jangling noise.

"Botts." He listened and then said, "Okay, sheriff. I'll call Mrs. Tanner and tell her you're coming."

Clark stubbed out his cigarette and walked over to the cop at the switchboard.

"Going out and check on things at Edward's Shack. I'll keep you posted." With that, Clark left the building.

Jackson could hear the engine of the patrol car as it left the parking lot.

"Officer Botts, tell Sheriff Mellichampe that I will call him later this afternoon."

In his blue rental, Jackson headed east out of town toward Edward's Lunch Shack.

CHAPTER 15

Mellichampe and the police photographer walked up to the Tanner house and rang the bell.

Cheryl Tanner opened the door, saw the sheriff and flew into a tirade, asking questions about why her husband was being held. Sheriff quieted her down and explained he wanted to take a few photos of tire marks made by her husband's pick-up.

"Why?"

"It could clear up this matter and free your husband."

Hearing that, she agreed.

The photographer took some excellent shots of tread track marks in the dirt driveway and also of the tires on the parked truck.

* * * * *

Clark did not head east on Highway 57, but north, out of town. Then he took the first left and drove west along the county road that bordered the Ryan and Crowder back property lines. He turned into the old logging road, drove up to the stream, and got out. He saw the fresh footprints made by the sheriff and the photographer in the damp, boggy ground.

So he's found this place. Smart ass.

He got back into his patrol car and drove west to the intersection, then south to the next intersection, then turned east on 57.

Wonder if she's home?

* * * * *

Patrick Ryan carefully got to his feet, walked over to Laura and put his one free arm about her.

"I have to go, now, but I'll call you later this afternoon. I know this has been a trying time for you, so why don't you get some rest."

"Yes, Patrick, I think I'll take a nap."

They kissed and Ryan went out, got into his car and left.

* * * * *

Ryan's car came out of Laura's driveway and turned east toward ERIN. Clark watched Ryan turn into his driveway, then he drove the patrol car east, back into Moultrie.

"Everything okay at the Shack?" Botts asked.

"Yeah. Very quiet." Clark lit a cigarette and passed the pack to Botts, who took one, lit it and puffed.

"Sheriff's at the Tanner place. Didn't say what he was doing."

"He never does until the last minute," Clark grumbled. "I'm going to get some lunch."

"Didn't get any at Edward's Shack?"

"I'm not eating with those Mexicans. They stink."

"If you're going to George's how about bringing me back a hamburger–loaded."

Clark left.

In town, people milled about, asking questions. When Clark got out of the patrol car a few grouped about him. They bombarded him with questions.

"Did they really find the bodies of Amelia Talbot and Sandra Perkins?"

"Did they get the person who did it?"

"Why did Cheryl's Beauty Salon close?"

"Was it Fred Tanner who was arrested?"

Clark pushed through the group and walked into George's Sandwich Shop. Seemed all the tables were full. People leaning toward each other in deep rumbling

166

discussion. He placed his order at the counter, turned and leaned back against it. His presence brought a quieting to the din.

Someone called out, "Hey, Jim, did they arrest Fred Tanner for killing Amelia Talbot and Sandra Perkins?"

"Can't say, but he's in lock-up."

The buzz of conversation grew loud. Clark picked up his order, paid the cashier, and got back into his patrol car.

At the police station, the two officers were eating their lunch when Roger Jackson came in.

"Went out to Edward's Lunch Shack and had lunch. Didn't see you there, Clark."

"No, I didn't go there."

Botts looked up at Clark. "Thought you said you did."

Jackson studied the officer's face, saw the healing cut on his cheek and asked, "How did you get the cut?" He pointed to his own cheek for designation.

"One of those migrants pulled a knife. Had to shoot him."

"You mean Carlos Cantu?"

Clark looked at Jackson. "You been askin' 'round?"

"I talked to a group of Mexicans while having lunch. They said Cantu never carried a knife."

"All them illegals carry knives." Clark took a bite of his burger and turned away. He glared at Botts until the man returned his attention to the switchboard. When finished, he stood and went out the door. They could hear the patrol car engine start up and leave.

Mellichampe and a man carrying a camera entered the station.

The sheriff looked at Botts. "Where's Clark."

"Just left."

"His pick-up out in the parking lot?"

"Guess so. He's in the patrol car."

Sheriff and the cameraman went out the door. A few minutes later they came back in and the cameraman took out the film cassette and left.

Mellichampe looked at Jackson, jerked his head toward his office, and Jackson got up and followed. The sheriff closed his office door.

* * * * *

Sue Bader called Laura around 2:30.

"Sounds like you're half asleep. Takin' a nap?"

"Oh, Sue, so much has happened. Can you find time to come out to my place this afternoon?"

"Be there in fifteen minutes," and true to her word, she was.

"Ya look a little peaked. What's wrong?"

Laura told Sue about finding evidence that someone was in her house, about the sheriff thinking it was someone after Laura, and the sheriff asking about her birthmark, which she quickly showed Sue.

"Who would know about that?"

"No one, except maybe Patrick."

Sue's eyebrows shot up. "Really? Guess you guys are getting along better than I thought."

Laura laughed and Sue joined in. "Great life, ain't it!"

Sue told Laura about the news going around town. About finding the bodies of Amelia Talbot and Sandra Perkins. Transporting them to the state corner's lab in Columbia. About Fred Tanner being arrested and Cheryl closing her shop.

"Do you have any plans for tonight?" Laura asked Sue.

"Nothing, really, just that Pete and I usually get together on Saturday nights. Why do you ask?"

Laura had been fighting her decision, giving herself many reasons not to say anything, but honesty won out. If she was to live in Moultrie, and face Patrick, Sue, and Pete, whom she had yet to meet, then she had to start on honest footing.

"I'd like you and Pete to come to the house this evening for dinner. I'm going to invite Patrick, also. Can you both come?"

"You betch-ya. What time?"

"Well, how about 7:00?"

"We'll be here." Sue got up. "Got to get home and call Pete. See you at 7:00."

After Sue Bader left Laura went to the phone and called Patrick.

"I know this is short notice but I'd like you to come over for dinner tonight, at 7:00. Sue Bader and her fiancé, Pete Harris, will be here too. Can you make it, Patrick?"

"Of course I can, Laura. You sound so mysterious."

" Nothing mysterious, just an honest revelation. See you at 7:00."

Laura got into her Mercedes, drove to the supermarket, and selected some prime steaks, a bag of salad fixings, firm, ripe tomatoes, a package of rolls to be baked, and a frozen cheesecake. She had potatoes at home and would bake them. She stopped by the ABC store and picked up two bottles of Robert Mondavi Merlot and headed home.

A rub of herbs and garlic powder was all the steaks needed. She set them aside, on a platter with tongs, to rest at room temperature. She scrubbed the potatoes, and had them ready to put in the oven. Next, in a large Wilton aluminum bowl, she tossed the salad and put it in the refrigerator.

The dining room was set with her mother's good china, crystal, and silverware. It was to be a special occasion. The outcome of which was uncertain. She could lose Patrick and also her friend, Sue. It could also mean that she would leave Moultrie. Sell everything and go back to Richmond. It was a chance she had to take.

She went upstairs to shower and dress.

* * * * *

Officer Clark observed the Bader car as it left Laura Crowder's place. Wonder if she's alone? Maybe I'll pay her a visit tonight.

* * * * *

Patrick was the first to arrive. He still used his cane but his walk was much improved. He brought a bottle of Frangelico.

"I see you're getting along great and thank you for thinking about the Frangelico." She took the bottle from him.

"Yes, I am, however I did take a pain pill before I left home."

She set the bottle on the foyer table, walked back to him and put her arms around his neck.

"Kiss me, Patrick."

"I don't need to be told that," and he folded his free arm about her waist and pulled her to him. His mouth covered hers with intense passion. "I need you, again, Laura."

"I need you, too, Patrick. I just hope you feel the same later this evening."

Patrick looked questioningly at her. "Why did you say that?"

"We'll see what the evening brings." She guided Patrick into the living room where he settled on the couch. A small tray of crackers and cheese was set out on the coffee table. "Help yourself. I'll be right back. Want to check on my potatoes." She picked up the bottle of liqueur and took it into the kitchen.

The door chimes sounded and Laura went to the door and steeled herself to come face-to-face with her half-brother. She opened the door and Sue burst through, a broad smile brightening her face.

"Laura, this is Pete Harris."

Laura lifted her eyes and stared into a pair of hazel eyes. It was almost like looking into her father's. It took her breath away. He was the image of her father in his early years.

170

The shock must have registered on her face for Sue put her hand on Laura's arm and said softly, "Laura?"

Laura quickly collected herself. "I, er, I'm very happy to meet you, Pete." She extended her hand.

The tall young man grasped her hand and shook it. "I'm so happy to meet you. Sue talks about you all the time. I've finally got to meet you."

Laura, remembering Patrick, turned toward him. "I don't know if you have met Patrick Ryan."

Sue nodded, "Yes, we've met. Patrick, this is my fiancé, Pete Harris."

Patrick got to his feet and took Harris's extended hand. "Yes, we've met before, right here in this house, as a matter of fact. At one of Judith's dinner parties."

"I remember, Mr. Ryan. Nice to see you again. What happened to your foot?"

"Turned it several days ago. Getting along nicely, though."

"What can I fix you to drink?" Laura walked to the wet bar.

Pete hurried behind her. "Here, I can do that."

"Thank you, Pete. I'll have a glass of Chardonnay. Fix Sue what she wants."

"Sue drinks bourbon," Pete said. "How about you, Mr. Ryan?"

"Scotch on the rocks will be fine."

Pete fixed the drinks, handed them out and sat across from Patrick, in the wing chair.

Sue and Laura took their drinks and Sue turned to Pete. "You guys settle down," she pointed to the cheese tray, "help yourself. I'll go help Laura in the kitchen." With that, the two women left the room.

When out of ear-shot Sue said, "You looked like you saw a ghost. Are you up to having us here?"

"Oh, yes, Sue. I'm fine, really." Laura moved to the oven, pierced a potato with a tester. "Almost ready." She slipped in the sheet of rolls to bake. "I'm planning on doing the steaks on the patio grill."

"Why not let Pete do that. He's very good at grillin'."

Laura thought for a moment. "Do you think he would mind?"

"Heck, no. He loves to get involved with the cookin'. He's a pretty good cook, himself."

With that, Sue spun around and got Pete.

"I'll be glad to grill them. As I recall, your dad had a gas grill out on the patio. I'll go out and check it." Pete pulled open the patio door, switched on the side patio lights, and stepped out on the patio.

"He seems to know where things are. I forget that he's been here before. Probably a couple of times."

"Indeed he has. Phillip used to bring him out for lunch, or a cook-out, or a dinner. Pete and I weren't dating at the time but he used to tell me about it at the office. Your dad and Pete were quite close."

Nervous twitches fluttered through Laura's stomach. *I hope I don't get cold feet. I have to go through with it.*

Patrick hobbled into the kitchen. "Since you've put Pete to work. Is there anything I can do?"

"Patrick, I don't think you should be on your feet so much. But since you're here, how about filling the water glasses with ice cubes. By the time we sit down there will be ice water."

Laura handed the ice bucket to Patrick, took out the salad bowl from the fridge, and followed him into the dining room. She heard Sue open the patio door and go out.

"Laura, you were a little startled meeting Pete. Is there anything wrong?"

"No, Patrick, it will be understandable later on this evening."

"You're acting mysteriously. Got something up your sleeve?"

"You might say that."

They returned to the kitchen and Sue stuck her head in. "How do you like your steaks?"

The response was mutual. "Rare."

Sue returned with the platter, washed it, dried it, and went back outside. In a few minutes Sue brought in the platter piled with the steaks and set it down. Pete followed.

Laura put the baked potatoes around the steaks, took out the baked rolls and placed them in a linen lined bread basket, and the foursome went into the dining room.

Patrick sat at the head of the table, Laura at the other end. Pete took the bottle of Merlot from the sideboard and filled the wine glasses then sat opposite Sue. The food was passed, family style, and they settled to enjoy the meal. They relaxed and sipped their wine, and let the conversation flow.

"Mr. Ryan..."

"Please call me Patrick."

"Er, Patrick, you probably know that I was raised by my mother. Her husband left her when I was born. I didn't realize until I was up in age that he probably left my mother because I was not his child."

"I heard something of the sort, yes."

"It's no secret to the town folks. They all seemed to know." He glanced at Laura. "Except you, Laura, not being from Moultrie." He took a sip of wine and continued. "I never knew my real father but I know that he was sending money to my mother for our support and later for my education. The other day I got a call from a lawyer in Columbia, Carleton Dinford, saying that an anonymous benefactor had left me some money and stocks. I know it had to be my true father because he never neglected my mother and me. I was flabbergasted when I heard the amount and I called Sue and asked her to marry me."

Sue looked with adoring eyes at Pete. "I was so happy, I said 'yes' immediately."

"I've been working for the County Planning Commission ever since I got out of college and I'll probably continue to work for the commission. And that's about the story of my life."

Laura pulled herself up straight in her chair. "Not quite, Pete."

All eyes turned to look at Laura. She saw the question marks on Sue's and Pete's face, but Patrick had a cool, unquestioning look. She stared at Patrick, and he nodded. *He knows. How did he know?*

Laura took a deep breath. "There's more to your life. You probably never gave a thought why Phillip and Judith Crowder, my mother and father, decided to settle here in Moultrie. Why he took a job with the beautification commission and saw you every day he worked. Why he invited you to the house so often." She saw Pete looking strangely at her. "Why he liked being around you." Laura got up, went to the sideboard and opened a draw, slid out a photograph and handed it to Pete.

Pete's eyes widened. The photograph was of Phillip Crowder in his early years. It was like looking at himself. He looked up at Laura and stared at her. She then handed Pete her father's letter to read. They all sat quietly as he read. When he finished he set the letter aside. "You could have overlooked his request. No one would have known."

"Except me," Laura said. "I wouldn't have been able to live with myself if I disregarded my father's last wishes."

Pete started to say something but his voice failed.

Sue looked at Pete then at Laura. "You mean that Phillip, your father, was Pete's father?"

"Yes." Laura looked at Patrick. "How did you know?"

"I had time to observe. Although Phillip was in his sixties, I could see the strong family resemblance. How much attention he paid to Pete. It was almost as though he wanted everyone to know. It was hard for him to hide how proud he was of Pete. I believe your mother knew or had some inkling.

"Yes, Mom knew.'"

Sue blurted, "Then you and Pete are related."

"He's my half-brother."

Sue clapped her hands. "Then when we marry you will be my sister-in-law."

Pete had managed to get his feelings under control, got up and came to Laura's side. He leaned down, put his arm about her shoulder and kissed her cheek. "I hope you won't be offended, but may I call you sis."

It was Laura's turn to fill up with emotion. She held back her tears. "I would love it."

Patrick loudly cleared his throat. "I suppose, my darling, that you have some dessert to serve."

It caught Laura by surprise and she laughed, and was joined by Sue and Pete. She had a happy, contented feeling as she realized she would not be leaving Moultrie, but had acquired more family.

* * * * *

It was raining when Sue and Pete left for home. Deputy Clark watched their car leave, and head toward Moultrie. He knew Ryan was still in Laura's house.

What's he waitin' for? That prick better not stay all night. If he does, I'll kill him.

Inside the house, Laura and Patrick talked while she cleaned up the dishes and put them in the dishwasher. They enjoyed another glass of Frangelico, put out all the lights on the lower floor, and went up the stairs to Laura's room.

Patrick entered Laura's room, looked about at the era displayed, the stuffed animals, diplomas hanging on the walls, and turned to her. "Your mother kept it just the way you left it for college."

"Yes. I haven't changed a thing."

He kicked off his loafers, and pulled her to him. "Help me undress, Laura."

She took his jacked off, Undid the top of his slacks and he stepped out of them, then she pulled the knit shirt up over his head and tossed it on her boudoir chair. His erection was pressing hard against his knit briefs.

Laura quickly rid herself of her clothing and helped Patrick into her full size bed.

"It's going to be a bit crowded. It's not like your king size bed," she chuckled.

"Don't need much space for what I'm going to do to you."

Laura sighed as they settled and Patrick pulled her to him with both arms. Her breasts flattened against his chest like two half-inflated balloons being pressed against a wall. He propped himself up on one elbow, bent down and kissed her strawberry birth mark just below her navel. His kisses traveled lower and his tongue flicked the sensitive nub within the soft hairs.

"Oh, Patrick, I wont be able to hold back if you keep that up."

"That's all right, my darling. We have all night to enjoy our bliss." With that, he plunged his tongue into her opening and enjoyed the sensations of her coming. Her cry of passion brought him up and upon her and he glided his rigidness into her wet entry. He pumped slowly, then accelerated, bringing on his own orgasm, and releasing his growl of satisfaction.

They renewed their passions by caressing each other's bodies, kissing and licking intimate places, then rode out their desires once again.

Both Laura and Patrick slept contentedly through what was left of the night.

Clark sat in his dark pick-up truck, cursing, as he watched the lights in Laura's room come on then in a few short minutes go off. There was no sign Patrick Ryan was leaving that night.

I'll kill that bastard.

He jammed the truck gear into "drive" and headed west toward a place where he knew he could get a cheap lay. His anticipation for Laura had built a rigid erection. He had to do something about it. He ripped along the highway and failed to notice the dark blue rental car that followed.

* * * * *

Sunday morning proved dismal outside. A light rain was still falling.

"April showers bring May flowers," whispered Laura into Patrick's ear. His smile lightened her heart.

Patrick swept his arms about her. "Last night, before we came to bed, you said you wanted a church wedding. Why don't we go and talk to Reverend Nicholson about setting a date?"

Laura inhaled deeply. It was a big step to take, but sooner or later it had to be taken. She slowly exhaled and nodded. "It's fine with me, Patrick, if you're up to it."

"I'll go home and change clothes." He picked up his watch from the night stand. "It's 9:30 now, Reverend Nicholson will be busy most of the morning with services. I'll give him a call to see if he could see us around 2:30. Meanwhile, why don't we go back to *Inn on the Square* in Greenwood for their buffet?"

"I'd like that. I enjoyed it last time."

"Good! I'll pick you up at 11:30." He pulled himself from the bed, dressed, and left.

CHAPTER 16

Over their Sunday luncheon buffet at *Inn on the Square* in Greenwood, they discussed the date for their wedding. Laura wanted to wait several months in respect for mourning her parents' death and Patrick agreed.

"I have to go to New York sometime soon and that's the only business trip I have planned. Would you like to come with me?"

"I don't think I'll have the time, Patrick, if we are going to be married in October. Invitations have to be printed and mailed out at least thirty days before the wedding and I will have to make a list. Wont be too many going out. I don't have any close friends. Then there's planning the reception. I think the country club would be the ideal place for that." She sighed, "There's much to do on the bride's side."

He nodded. "Another thing I can take care of, give me the key to your Richmond apartment in Baxter's Mill and I will stop there on my way back from New York and make arrangements to have your belongings moved down to Moultrie."

"That would be wonderful. Can you do that?"

"Of course!"

They drove back to Moultrie and arrived at the manse to talk to Reverend Nicholson, who marked his calendar and reserved the church for the occasion. October 10th.

At home, Laura found a phone message from Sue saying what a wonderful time they had Saturday night and Pete was so excited about having a sister. Laura could hear the happiness in Sue's voice and it made her happy.

* * * * *

Wednesday, ankle much improved, Patrick Ryan drove through town headed toward Columbia.

Laura drove into town, stopped by Caper's and brought her up-to-date on revealing to Pete Harris about being her half-brother and the plans for her wedding

"How did Pete take the news?"

"He's happy about it. Seems he was very fond of my father."

"Yes, that's what your mother told me just before they left."

Laura's eyes filled. "I wish Mom and Dad were here to see me get married in October."

"October. Beautiful month for a wedding," Caper said. "Bridesmaids' gowns in deep fall colors. I can see it now." Caper was excited.

I don't think I'll have any bridesmaids. Perhaps a maid-of-honor."

"Whatever you say. Are you traditional when it comes to a wedding gown?"

"Yes, I guess I am. I want something plain but chic, with a finger-tip veil."

"Your wish is my command. I will contact my suppliers and have them send me pictures of their fall offerings." Caper hugged Laura. "I'm so excited you'd think I was the one getting married."

Laura laughed. "I'm getting cold feet. I hope I can get through this." *In more ways than one.*

"Not to worry, you'll come through with flying colors."

When Laura left Caper's she paid no notice to the deputy's patrol car across from her parked Mercedes.

Police officer James Clark watched her leave the shop.

I'll bide my time. Saw Ryan headed out of town so he's out of the picture. Now it's my turn.

* * * * *

179

Laura stopped by the office of the *Moultrie Monitor* and asked if they did specialized printing such as wedding invitations. They did, and showed her their portfolio. She spent a lengthy time looking through the book and jotting down the catalog numbers of several that interested her. She would have to consult Patrick for his input.

She drove home, her mind whirling with excitement of her up-coming wedding, never noticing she was being followed by a pick-up truck.

* * * * *

Jackson drove his rental past Laura's place, saw no pick-up, turned around and drove to the entrance of ERIN. His eye noticed the electrical sensor in the pillars on each side of the driveway. *Too dark last time to notice them. At least Ryan will know I'm coming in.*

Patrick Ryan was standing out front. He looked both agitated and anxious.

Jackson parked his car and got out.

"I want to go with you, Roger."

"No way, Mr. Ryan. This is police work and we don't need civilians in the middle of it. Besides, I think Clark will wait until dark before he makes a move. He's chicken shit."

Patrick nodded his head. "I'll do as you say, Roger."

The tall muscular black man, dressed entirely in black, nodded. "Good! I'm going over there now. It's going to be a long night." He took off toward the edge of the road and vanished.

* * * * *

Sheriff Mellichampe drove past the Crowder house. Behind him was a patrol car with two "rookies". He saw there was no pick-up truck in front of the Crowder house so he eased his car to the shoulder of the road and parked. The trailing patrol car did the same.

"You okay, Sheriff?" came over his radio.

"Yeah, he radioed back. "Got to think." He lit a cigarette, took a few puffs, then stared at the cigarette, smashed it out and radioed the patrol car. "You men follow me."

They took a right at the intersection, then another right. He pulled over to the side of the road near the old logging road. He got out, walked back to the patrol car and said, "Wait here, I'll be right back."

When he got about fifty yards down the logging road he saw the rear of Clark's pick-up. He went back to the patrol car.

"I want you both to listen carefully." He handed his car keys to one of the officers. "You take my car and you both drive back to the Crowder place. I want you to pull in the driveway, just off the road, and sit there. Don't get out. If you see some strange things going on just observe. I have a trap I'm setting and I don't want you two in the middle. Do nothing until I wave for you to come up. Is that clear?"

"Yes sir," they said in unison. One of them said, "But, sheriff, why are we here?"

"For backup and, hopefully, to take a prisoner to lock-up."

The two cars drove off and Sheriff Mellichampe walked back on the logging road. He noticed the light was fading and glanced at his watch. It was 7:30.

* * * * *

In the kitchen, Laura unloaded the dishwasher. She rubbed her arms from the fearful chill she felt. *Will it work?*

She selected a few leftovers from the fridge, warmed them in the microwave oven and slowly dined on the food. Her ears listening for any unusual sounds. In truth, she was scared. Would the intruder come back? How would she protect herself? As those thoughts whirled through her mind, she got up and put her dishes in the dishwasher. She glanced out the window. Even though it was after 8 o'clock there was still enough light left to make out the woods line. Daylight Savings Time. She took a long look at the knife block and shook her head. *No weapon.*

She went through the lower floor of the house and turned off the lights. With heavy feet she climbed the stairs and went into her bedroom. In the bathroom, she slipped into her nightgown, brushed her teeth and used the commode, ever listening for a sound. She heard none. When she came out of the bathroom she was staring into the eyes of Officer Clark

He was not in uniform. Clark had already removed his shirt and his bare chest revealed a heavy growth of chest hairs. They were repulsive to Laura.

"What the hell are you doing here?" she screamed at him.

"I'm going to do just what that Ryan does to you." He jabbed his finger in the direction of ERIN. "Got any objections?"

Laura, realizing she was wearing just a nightgown, reached for her robe on the back of the bathroom door.

Clark pushed the door back. "You won't need it."

She crossed her arms over her breasts and mustered up her most forceful voice. "Get the hell out of my house."

He reached for her arm and Laura pulled back. "Don't you touch me, you pig."

"Oh, it was all right for me to help you with your groceries. That was fine, wasn't it Miz Crowder. You didn't object to that." He rubbed his hand over the bulge of his zippered fly. "Now I'd like a little help from you."

"You mean the same help you gave Amelia Talbot and Sandra Perkins?"

Clark's head pulled up. "Smart ass, ain't you. Figured it out all by yourself. I was just gonna fuck you but now it's another story. When I get through with you I'll dump your body down by the Mexican housing."

"You mean you're not going to hide me in the lake like you did the others?"

"Can't. They know of those places."

He opened his fly and freed his strong erection. Grabbing Laura, he ripped the light nightgown from her body and threw her upon her bed. He was very strong and she was no match for him.

He ran his finger over the strawberry birth mark just below her navel. "It's nice to see it up close and not through binoculars."

A scream left her throat as he climbed upon her.

"Scream all you want. Ain't nobody around to hear you." He pressed his forearm into her neck cutting off her air.

Laura scratched at his face.

"Regular hell-cat." His hand slid down to his side and came up with his hunting knife. "You don't lay still and I'll cut your throat right now."

Laura stared at the huge knife and its toothed edge. It took all the resistance out of her. "No, please don't kill me. I'll do what you say."

"That's more like it." He slid the knife back into his hip sheath. "Now, open your legs, baby, 'cause I'm going to fuck you all night."

A powerful black log-of-an-arm came about Clark's neck and he was lifted bodily off Laura. The other muscular arm tossed the sheet over her exposed body.

"Say what? you skinny white trash." The tall black man shook Clark like a rag doll.

Another voice was heard. Sheriff Mellichampe was standing right behind the black man. "Let me cuff him, Jackson. He has to be my take."

The tall black man named Jackson spun Clark around so the sheriff could handcuff him. While Mellichampe read Clark his "rights", Jackson patted down Clark looking for any other weapons. Finding none, he removed the hunting knife from its sheath, picked up Clark's shirt and wrapped the weapon in it.

The sheriff unbuckled Clark's belt and pulled it through the pant loops. The knife sheath fell to the floor. Mellichampe picked it up, thought for a moment, then handed it to

Roger Jackson. "Put this with the knife. I'll send both to the lab in Columbia."

Laura was breathing heavily as she watched the scene unfold before her eyes. "God, I'm so glad to see you, sheriff, but I don't know this man."

Sheriff Mellichampe looked at Jackson. "This is the private investigator Ryan called in from New York. His name is Roger Jackson. He turned up some interesting information that was very useful in our investigation of the missing women. He was also the king pin in Ryan's plan tonight."

"Patrick didn't tell me about him." Laura slipped out of bed wrapped in the sheet and went into the bathroom and retrieved her robe and put it on.

When she came out Patrick burst through the door of the bedroom. He raced to her.

"Laura, are you okay?"

She fell into his arms. "I am now."

Patrick softly rubbed her back to ease her shaking. "I hated to use you as bait but you were so agreeable to it. The plans we made Saturday night worked out fine."

"I thought I told you to stay put," Jackson said to Ryan.

"Couldn't. I had to come over."

Jackson shook his head. "Glad you didn't come too soon. It could have ruined everything."

Laura looked up at Patrick. "How did you get word to him without Clark knowing?"

"Let me tell her, just give me time to get this vermin into the waiting patrol car and get him to the jail," sheriff said and both he and Jackson hustled Clark down the stairs and outside.

Laura and Patrick followed them down and Laura went into the kitchen and put on a fresh pot of coffee.

Mellichampe waved the officers to drive up. The two "rookies" stared at Clark, their fellow police officer, now in the sheriff's custody. Bare-chested, pants hanging loosely on his hips with the fly gaping open, he made quite a sight. They shook their heads in disbelief as sheriff pushed Clark into the back of the patrol car and slammed the door.

Mellichampe went to his car, reached in for the radio microphone. "Botts, tell Detective Campbell to release Fred Tanner and drive him home. Be sure to tell Tanner that I said 'thanks' for his help. You got that?"

"Yes sir."

The sheriff turned toward the two young police officers now sitting in the patrol car. "You take this piece of shit and lock him up. I gave him the Miranda." He took the wrapped sheath and knife from Jackson and handed it to one of the men. "Lock this up in the Evidence Room and then give the shirt back to Clark. Don't want him to catch cold before his trial."

"Yes sir."

Sheriff rapped on the roof of the car and the two officers drove off. Then he and Jackson went back into the house and, by following the aroma of fresh coffee, found the kitchen.

"Believe me, it's been one hellish night," he said as he dropped into a kitchen chair. "First of all, Ryan called me on a pretense of business and we, generally, laid out the plans to trap Clark. I," he glanced up at Jackson, "and Jackson knew Clark was our man but we had no evidence. It's true the tire treads matched those found at the scene where Amelia Talbot disappeared but that wouldn't hold water against a slick lawyer. Even BB would laugh at that."

Laura looked askance at Patrick.

"Butler Brown."

"Anyway, when I got back to the office yesterday I casually mentioned that Ryan was going out of town today and wanted someone to keep an eye on his property since there appeared to be a break-in at Miss Crowder's on April 30th.

"What threw us off was his truck not being parked in front of the house here. He played that pretty cool. He came from the other side of the field back of the house. Drove in on the old logging road from the road that borders on the north side of your property," he looked at Laura, "where you found cigarette butts."

She nodded her head. "Then he came across the field and probably came through the patio doors."

"He did," Jackson stated.

Mellichampe looked at Jackson, then said, "I'll check the doors later."

Laura got out cups, cream and sugar and poured the coffee. Sheriff took a big swig of the black brew. "Mmm, that's good."

Laura sat next to Patrick and the sheriff directed his talk to them.

"As I said, it threw me when I saw no car, but then when I lit a cigarette I remembered the logging road. We drove around there and in on the road we saw his old pick-up truck. I knew he crossed the field, so I sent my guys driving both cars back to the front of the house and I ran across the field. Came to the front of the house just as Jackson was picking the lock on the front door." He turned toward Roger Jackson. "Say, just where were you to get here so quickly?"

"My rental is parked in Ryan's driveway. I was here when Miss Crowder came home. I also saw Clark's pick-up pass by the driveway, going west. I had to mull that over."

"When did you first realize Clark was in the house?"

"I wasn't stationary. I circled the house once every hour. Saw the little weasel as he was entering through the patio doors. It was hard for me to wait, to give Clark time to face Miss Crowder. That was the risky part. I got to the front of the house and started to pick the lock, when you arrived," he nodded toward the sheriff.

"Why didn't you go through the patio doors like Clark did?"

"He knew the layout of the house from when he broke in on the 30th. I'm not familiar with the interior and my pen light wouldn't help much. I chose the front door and foyer because most staircases to the upper landing are in the foyer."

Sheriff nodded and continued, "When we got in I followed Jackson up the stairs, heard your scream," he glanced at Laura, "and Jackson took off like a shot, taking three steps at a time."

Laura gave an involuntary shiver and Patrick put his arm about her shoulders.

"We heard him say what he planned to do with your body. You were pretty cool to keep him talking about where he hid the bodies of Amelia Talbot and Sandra Perkins. Jackson, here, waited until he sheathed his knife before he went in. He knew if he busted in while Clark was holding the knife he would have time to cut your throat. As soon as the knife was back in the sheath Jackson shot over, picked Clark up like he was nothing, and I followed in. The rest you know."

Laura, still shaking, said, "It was pretty close. I had to keep him talking, I didn't know when the cavalry would arrive."

Sheriff Mellichampe gave a chuckling snort and nodded to Patrick. "Told you she has guts." He got up, said he'd play down the particulars in his report, shook all three outstretched hands and left.

Jackson got up. "Guess I'll mosey along to my Nam buddy's home. Be leaving in the morning. Sheriff said to send my bill to him and he'd personally see that it was taken care of a.s.a.p." He turned to Laura. "Don't forget to send me a wedding invitation." He shook Patrick's hand and leaned toward Laura. "Do you mind, little lady, if I give you a hug?"

"I'd be insulted if you didn't."

Jackson hugged Laura, turned and left.

Laura dropped back into her chair. "What an evening. I'm still a bit rattled."

"I'll stay the night with you so you feel a bit safe."

Laura nodded. "I'd like that, Patrick."

Cradled in Patrick's arms, she slept like a baby.

* * * * *

CHAPTER 17

Roger Jackson had packed his bag the night before. He was ready to go home. He carried the bag downstairs to the front door. Joellyn came from the kitchen munching salted crackers.

"I hope you and Lorine will come to visit us."

"You can bet on that, Joellyn. You and Lorine would get along just fine." He looked about. "Where's Chuck?"

"He's outside talking to some of his workers. He'll be in in a few minutes."

"Just wanted to say how much I enjoyed being with you and Chuck. You're going to make him very happy. Don't forget to send me an announcement."

Joellyn looked at him with surprise. "How did you know? I haven't even told Charles yet."

"You forget, Joellyn, Lorine and I have two children. I saw you munching on crackers trying to ward off morning sickness."

Joellyn smiled. "Should be sometime in November. Don't worry, I'll send you an announcement."

Godwin came in from the kitchen. "Sure hate to see you go, ol' buddy, but it's been a pleasure having you with us. Hope you and Lorine will come..."

"I already told him that they better come down to see us."

Godwin walked over and put his arm around his wife and kissed her on the cheek. "Ain't she something."

It was a statement to which Roger Jackson agreed. "Sure is." He picked up his clothing bag, packed it in the dark blue rental, shook Godwin's hand, kissed Joellyn on the cheek, waved "goodbye", and was gone.

* * * * *

Sheriff Mellichampe looked into the conference room. "Where in the hell did all those reporters come from?"

"Around the state. You're big news, sheriff."

"The hell I am."

The young officer continued, "Seems word got out about the capture of the killer."

"'Word got out', and how did that happen?"

The officer looked sheepish. "Now sheriff, you know this is a small town. Word spreads fast."

"Yeah, yeah, I know. Can't keep a lid on anything."

Sheriff Mellichampe straightened his shoulders, pulled open the door to the conference room and entered. There was an immediate quieting as all eyes followed the sheriff to the front of the room. Several microphones had been set up and the sheriff scowled, took out a small piece of paper and read from it.

"I wish to announce that we have in custody the perpetrator we believe is responsible for the murders of Amelia Talbot and Sandra Perkins." He turned and started to walk away.

"Sheriff, is it Fred Tanner?"

Sheriff Mellichampe spun around. "Absolutely not! We took Tanner in custody for his protection as he was instrumental in pointing us in the direction of the killer. As soon as the killer was in custody we took Tanner home. Tanner is a dedicated citizen of this county and a volunteer for our county fire department. In my eyes he's a hero."

The rumble and shuffling of feet and paper filled the room. A voice from the rear asked, "Who are you holding, sheriff?"

Mellichampe stared, without seeing. "A rogue cop, Officer Jim Clark. Good day, gentlemen," and he marched out of the room as the din behind him grew louder and vociferous.

In his office, Sheriff Mellichampe told Detective Campbell to impound Clark's truck.

"Yes, sir. What about the knife and the tarpaulin in the back of the truck?"

"Send them to the State Lab. I have an idea we'll find confirmation of charges on those items."

* * * * *

Laura and Patrick sat in the kitchen eating breakfast.

"Can you imagine what it must be like in town this morning?" Patrick said. "People will be everywhere, huddling together and expressing their concerns. It'll be a mad house."

"Thank goodness, we don't have to go into town."

* * * * *

The rugged barrel-chested man got up from his office chair and went out to the front desk.

"Botts, did you call over to George's Sandwich Shop and have them send over lunch for Clark?"

"No, sheriff, I didn't think of it."

Sheriff Mellichampe shook his head. "Prisoner could die of starvation in that cell downstairs if you guys were running the station. But I wouldn't much care this time. Call over."

He resettled in the wooden office chair and could hear Botts on the phone. At noon, the delivery from George's arrived and sheriff got up, unhooked the jail cell key from the key board and led the way downstairs.

When Mellichampe turned in the direction of the jail cell he saw that it was empty, door open.

"Damn it!"

He raced up the stairs and faced the two "rookies". "Which one of you locked up Clark last night?"

"We both did, sheriff."

"Did you search him?"

"Yes, sir. There wasn't anything in his clothes. We even took his shoe laces."

"Did you check his shoes?"

The two young officers looked at each other then back at the sheriff. "No sir. Thought he'd need his shoes on that cold cement floor."

"Botts, put out an APB now," Mellichampe ordered. "Include the State Police. Clark has flown the coop."

The two young "rookies" stared at the angry man with bulging eyes. "How'd he do that, sheriff?"

"Must have had a key. Most likely in his shoe. I'd say he escaped when all the newspaper reporters were in the conference room. Everyone was in there," he looked around, "including the staff. In all that excitement, he made a clean get-away. Gees, my name will be mud."

Mellichampe saw the package from George's sitting on the outer counter and swung his head around to look out the window. He saw the delivery kid entering the sandwich shop and knew in a matter of minutes the news would be all over town. He shook his head.

"I guess, by now he's out of the state," mumbled one young officer.

Mellichampe's head came up. His brow furrowed in thought then he dropped into a chair. The two "rookies" watched as the big man's eyes glazed over in deep thought.

"No. No, I don't think so," he said slowly and softly.

"You mean he's still in Moultrie?"

"Yes, I think so, but just which one would he pick?"

The young officers stared at their boss as if he had lost his mind.

The front door opened and Detective Campbell rushed in.

"Sheriff, I took Clark's truck to the compound but when I walked back Clark's patrol car was missing. Where is it?"

Sheriff nodded. "Guess Clark took it."

"Clark? I thought he was downstairs in the cell."

"Was," and explained to Campbell what he thought happened. "Botts, look up Fred Tanner's phone number, call him and tell him what happened."

"Tell Tanner?"

"Yes. Clark may go after him for revenge. Tell him to lock up and keep his family safe."

Botts did so quckly.

Who else would he go after? "Call the Crowder residence and tell Miss Crowder the same thing. Also Patrick Ryan."

* * * * *

The police patrol car crunched up the dirt and gravel road and stopped in front of the river cottage. Clark got out, hoisted up his belt-less pants, went to the door and rapped. He looked about and seeing no one tried the door knob. The door opened and he went in, closing the door behind him.

Zeke Mills was nowhere to be found.

Little shit must be on the creek fishing.

Clark opened a closet, found a flannel shirt and a belt, put them on and left his old shirt on the floor. In the kitchen, he felt the coffee pot and found it stone cold. *Musta gone out last night.* He selected a large, sharp knife from the rack, settled in the only chair in the front room and waited.

He heard Zeke Mills approach the rear of the cottage. Peeking out the window, Clark watched him slap down a string of fish on the outside gutting board, clean the fish and dump the offal into the creek. With the fish in a tin pan, Zeke Mills headed for the back door of his kitchen--and his death.

* * * * *

After receiving the call from police headquarters, Patrick, taking Blarney with him, went over to Laura's place to be with her. He didn't want her to be alone with this killer on the loose.

Thursday afternoon Sheriff Mellichampe toured the town in his patrol car, giving every pedestrian a quick study. He knew that by now the townspeople heard of Clark's escape. The saying "news travels fast in a small town" is no joke. Much to his chagrin he knew this morning's reporters also heard.

He wracked his brain trying to figure out where Clark would go. He had already checked Clark's house. The patrol car wasn't there.

A patrol car would be hard to hide. Have to be in a wooded area.

He drove past the Ryan and Crowder rear property lines and didn't see any change in the crime scene tapes closing the logging road behind the Crowder place. He realized they could have been untied and replaced but he didn't believe Clark was stupid enough to return to where his truck was found.

Has to be a wooded area with access. Just how many of those do we have in the county?

He pulled over and stopped his patrol car, lit a cigarette, and mentally scanned the county roads. He crushed out the cigarette stub, crossed his arms over his broad chest, and dropped his head to think. His head came up, and with his thick brows knitted tightly, he drove the car out onto the road and headed for Zeke Mills' river cottage.

I mentioned Zeke Mills' place when I called in for the Search and Recovery Team. I'm sure Clark heard this over a scanner. I just hope the old man is okay.

Sheriff saw the fresh tire tracks as he drove into Zeke's place and feared the worst. He found Zeke's body in the kitchen. Throat cut. Exactly like the two women who had been murdered. A pan of fresh fish set in the sink. He threw the kitchen chair against the back door in anger and frustration, and went out to his car to call Botts at police headquarters.

* * * * *

Dr. Lyon, the county coroner examined Zeke Mills'
body, pronounced it a homicide, and left. The body was then
removed by a local mortician and taken to the state morgue.

Mellichampe was pissed-off. He had to find Clark before he killed anyone else. He got into his patrol car and
drove east on Highway 57. His brain clicked as he passed the
entrance to the old hunting trail. Being no cars behind him,
he backed up and pulled onto the rutted road. He got out,
walked a bit along the road, looking for tire marks. About a
hundred yards into the wooded area he spied old tracks and a
section of ground stained dark. Examining it closer he
determined the stain to be the residual of blood. He went
back to his car, called in to headquarters and asked Botts to
tell Detective Campbell to come to the old hunting road
where he would be waiting, and to bring the forensic kit.

* * * * *

Clark drove along a county road north of Moultrie, took
a crossroad and drove to the rear of his house. He put on his
police uniform and noticed the holster was empty. Mellichampe had been there and removed the pistol. He went out
to the small shed in the backyard, retrieved a revolver from a
cardboard box on a shelf, and jammed it into his holster.

He drove up to the county road and headed west. He
planned on paying Patrick Ryan a visit. He drove into the
entrance of ERIN and slowly moved along the curving
driveway to the front of the house. Because the driveway
curved, it would be impossible to see the police car from the
road.

The security photo-eye alerted Robert and he opened
the front door before Clark could ring the bell.

"Yes, sir, can I help you?"

"My name is Detective Campbell, Moultrie Police Department. Is Mr. Ryan home?"

"No, sir, he ain't."

"Can you reach him?"

"Yes, sir, I know where he is."

"Good. Is there anyone else in the house at this time?"

"Only my wife, Miz Taylor. She's in the kitchen."

"Call her out."

"I can't do that Detective Campbell."

"Why?"

"She wouldn't hear me. She's deaf. I have to go fetch her."

"Then do it."

Robert studied the tense face before him and his brow knitted. "Is there something wrong, Detective Campbell?"

Clark was antsy. A nervous twitch clicked at the edge of his eye.

Robert saw the anxious state of the man and began to worry.

"Perhaps I could have Miz Taylor fix you a cup of coffee."

"I'm not here to socialize." He pulled the gun from his holster and pointed it at Robert. "You lead the way, I'll follow."

Robert stared at the gun then up at Clark. He was frightened and realized this man was not Detective Campbell but had to be the escapee, Clark. Ryan received a phone call from the police, notifying him of Clark's escape, and went immediately over to Laura Crowder's to be with her. Now the murderer was here, in the house.

He turned and led the way to the kitchen where his wife was making preparations for dinner. She looked up at her husband, saw the fear in his eyes, then at Clark and saw the mean intent upon his face and the gun pointed at her husband. She dropped the bag of potatoes on the floor.

Robert swiftly bent and scooped up the bag and placed it on the counter. He put his arm about his wife's shoulders and guided the tall, stately woman out of the kitchen.

They assembled in the living room and Clark, waving the gun menacingly, instructed Robert to make the call to Ryan.

"Ya better make it good so's he comes home immediately."

Robert dialed the Crowder residence and Laura picked up the phone.

"Miz Crowder, may I speak with Mr. Pat?" When Ryan got on the phone Robert said, "Mr. Pat, there's a Detective Campbell here from the Moultrie Police, and he wants to talk to you. Can you come home now?"

Ryan frowned. This wasn't Robert's way or manner. He was about to ask if anything was wrong when Robert added, "And if you don't mind, Mr. Pat, could you swing by the drug store and pick up Miz Taylor's prescription, she's been having a spell or two lately." He hung up the phone.

"What's this shit about a prescription?" Clark growled.

"I took the prescription there yesterday. My wife has trouble with her gall bladder. Mr. Ryan knows that."

Clark waived the gun to indicate Robert sit. Mrs. Taylor was already seated on the sofa and Robert sat beside her and took her hand in his.

"Now, we'll wait," Clark sneered.

* * * * *

Ryan put the phone back in its cradle and stared at Laura. "Something's wrong at the house. That was Robert calling to tell me that a Detective Campbell was there and wants to talk to me."

Laura's eyes widened.

"He also asked me to go by the drug store and pick up Mrs. Taylor's prescription. Mrs. Taylor hasn't been sick a day in her life. Something is definitely wrong. I have to go, Laura."

Laura put her hand out to stop Patrick. "Before you go, call police headquarters and see if they know anything about Detective Campbell wanting to speak with you."

Ryan did so.

Botts said, "Mr. Ryan, Detective Campbell is with Sheriff Mellichampe out on the county road. I don't understand this."

Ryan said, "Do me a favor, Mr. Botts. Please call Sheriff Mellichampe and tell him what's going on. I have to go to the house as Robert and Mrs. Taylor may be in danger." He hung up the phone, gave Laura a kiss, and went out and got in his car, calling back over his shoulder, "Laura, keep the doors locked, and Blarney close, until I come back." The low sports car threw up some gravel as the tires grabbed to move quickly.

* * * * *

Clark watched as the sports car purred to the front of the house and parked. He saw Ryan reach for a small bag, and get out.

"Probably the prescription," Clark surmised. He tensed and clasped the gun tighter. He could feel the sheen of sweat on his brow and upper lip and wiped them with his sleeve.

CHAPTER 18

Mellichampe watched Campbell gather specimens of stained earth and grass and put them in plastic bags. He heard Botts' voice calling him on the police car radio. He got in the car and picked up the receiver.

"Yeah, Botts, what's up?"

Botts told sheriff what Ryan had said. Supposedly, a Detective Campbell was at Ryan's house and wanted to question him, and that Ryan was at the Crowder house but would go to his house immediately.

"I'm on my way to Ryan's." He turned, called Campbelll to get in his car and follow him to Ryan's, and jammed the car into gear and shot out onto Highway 57.

It's got to be Clark.

He picked up his radio transmitter and said, "Campbell, let's do this quietly. I believe Clark is at Ryan's place. I want to surprise him."

"Okay, sheriff.

The two patrol cars moved swiftly through town heading west out of Moultrie.

* * * * *

Patrick braced himself as he pushed open the front door. With a quick glance he took in Mrs. Taylor and Robert sitting on the couch. Robert was holding his wife's trembling hands, their faces tense with fear. Clark was standing in front of them waving a gun.

Clark turned and sneered, "Well, the lover boy has returned."

"What the hell do you think you're doing, Clark?"

"I'm gonna finish what I started, but first, I'm gonna get rid of you. Another killin' wont matter much."

A long, eerie wail filled the room as Mrs. Taylor slowly got up and clutched her side. She ran her fingers through her pepper-salt hair and doubled over, as if in pain, and placed her hands on the coffee table.

The movement threw Clark off-guard and he was torn between whom he should aim the gun. He stepped back to have a wider perspective.

Mrs. Taylor shoved the coffee table against the side of Clark's legs, throwing him off-balance.

Patrick Ryan jumped at Clark, knocking the gun out of his hand. It skittered across the Oriental rug between the two opposing couches and slid out onto the oak flooring.

Clark grabbed Ryan about the neck with both hands, bending him backwards. Ryan kicked at Clark's legs connecting with a shin. They both fell to the floor in a contorted mass of flailing fists.

Robert went swiftly to retrieve the gun and placed the barrel against Clark's head.

"Let loose of Mr. Ryan, or I'll pull the trigger."

The command had little effect upon Clark as he continued to bash Ryan with his fists. His face twisted with hatred as he pulled out Zeke Mills' kitchen knife and raised it.

Robert pulled the trigger.

The vibration of the fired bullet shocked Mrs. Taylor, who was now standing, she saw what happened and went to her husband and stood by his side.

Mellichampe burst through the front door, visually took in the scene, and removed the gun from Robert's hand. He gave the elderly black man's shoulder a gentle squeeze.

Detective Campbell helped Patrick to his feet. "That was a close call, Mr. Ryan."

"Yes, it was but thanks to Robert here, I'm all right."

Mellichampe shook Robert's hand. "You saved the county a lot of money. We would have had to hold a trial that would have ended exactly the same. Clark's death."

Robert lowered his head and his wife put her arm about his waist and lay her head against his chest.

Laura's car screeched to a halt in front of Patrick's home. She dashed into the house almost colliding with Detective Campbell.

"Patrick? Where are you?"

"In here, Laura. I'm okay."

She rushed into his arms and hugged him. "My God, Patrick, I was so worried about you coming over here." She glanced down and saw the body of Jim Clark. "Why did he come here?"

"Evidently, to kill me."

Laura hugged him tighter.

Sheriff Mellichampe walked over to the phone on the open bar and punched in numbers.

"Mellichampe here. Tell Doc Lyon to come to the Ryan place. Got another body for him. Jim Clark was shot."

Laura looked at Robert, who was visibly shaken, and then saw, for the first time, Mrs. Taylor. The tall, stately black woman stood next to her husband. Her face reflecting pride and love. She walked over to the woman and hugged her.

"I'm so glad Robert was here to save Patrick."

Robert said softly, "Miz Crowder…"

"Please, Robert, call me Laura."

"Miz Laura, Mrs. Taylor can't hear you. She's deaf."

Laura pulled back her head and stared into Mrs. Taylor's eyes. "I think she knows what I said."

Tears glistened in both women's eyes.

Mellichampe cleared his throat. "Doc Lyon will be here soon to check the body, then we'll have it removed." He turned to Robert. "You can get back to whatever you were doing before this happened."

Robert put his arm about his wife's shoulder and led her out of the living room.

Laura watched the couple leave. She couldn't help but think how much Mrs. Taylor resembled the well-noted chef, Edna Lewis. The same aristocratic look and bearing. She shook her head in amazement.

* * * * *

Long before the sun went down, the townspeople of Moultrie heard of Clark's attack on Ryan and how Clark was killed.

The next day Sue Bader called Laura. "Just heard about Clark getting' killed at Patrick's house. Are you okay?"

"Yes, but Patrick was almost killed." Laura heard Sue gasp. "But he's okay thanks to Robert. Robert Killed Clark."

"Who's Robert?"

"Patrick's butler."

"Oh my God, how did that happen?"

"Clark came to Patrick's house while Patrick was here, with me. It's a long story. Can you come to the house for lunch and I'll tell you about it."

"You bet."

* * * * *

Abstractly, Sue stirred her coffee while listening to Laura tell of her night's experience with Clark and how Sheriff Mellichampe and a Mr. Jackson came charging in to her bedroom to rescue her. Then the news that Clark escaped jail, and how Robert called Patrick to come home.

"The rest I was told by Patrick. How Mrs. Taylor ran the coffee table into Clark's legs. Patrick fighting with Clark. Robert got the gun and shot Clark dead."

"This is almost like Millie's experience with the exchange murderer."

"You said you would tell me about you and Millie and that murderer. Now's as good a time as any."

So Sue Bader told Laura all about Worldwide Time-shares where she worked in Cleveland, Ohio, the thesis Millie was writing, how she and Millie met at Shipyard Plantation, and how they figured out about the murders taking place at the timeshare resorts.

"You'll meet her. She and Bob are coming down for my wedding."

"Speaking about your wedding, how are your plans going?"

"Just fine. We're not havin' a big bash. Just a simple church wedding. Believe it or not, we're gonna have the reception in George's back meeting room. I'm only invitin' about fifty people. I don't know many folks since I've been in Moultrie less than a year."

"Doesn't make much difference how many you invite, The main thing is you'll be married. Where will you live after you're married?"

"In Pete's house. It's a nice little home and it's fully furnished. Old pieces, but good ones."

"Sounds good. I'm still working on my wedding plans."

"Have you decided what you're gonna do with your home here?"

"No, not yet. I think Patrick will advise me on that."

The two women finished their lunch, cleaned up the dishes, and Sue went back to the planning commission's office.

* * * * *

True to his word, Patrick made all the arrangements and had Laura's furnishings moved to Moultrie. The small amount was stored in her garage.

She was delighted to have her clothing once again.

Her license to practice law in South Carolina was granted and she became a member of the South Carolina Bar Association. She would think about where to establish her law office.

Patrick further advised Laura that his son, Kevin, would be spending some summer time with him and should arrive in July.

Laura became apprehensive. *What if he doesn't like me, would this come between Patrick and me?*

CHAPTER 19

June 27th was a beautiful day for Sue's wedding. It was held in the Rock Church of the Lord just east of Moultrie. The assemblage belied Sue's statement of not knowing many people. Evidently, Pete was pretty well known.

Laura stepped into the anteroom where Sue and her Matron of Honor, Millie Sutherland were preparing for the ceremony.

Sue was radiant in her simple white satin gown and finger-tip veil and Laura went to her and kissed her cheek.

"Laura, this is my friend, Millie Sutherland from Harrisonburg, Virginia."

The two women shook hands. Laura was surprised to see that Millie was in the early stage of pregnancy. Her complexion glowed, her dark hair gleamed, and the pink of her gown enhanced her beauty. She realized how easily Patrick could have been attracted to her.

"I'm very glad to meet you, Millie. I've heard so much about you from Sue."

"And I heard a lot about you, Laura. Seems we both had narrow escapes from murderers. We'll have to get together and compare notes."

"Sounds good to me," Laura chuckled. She gave Sue another hug. "I'll see you after the ceremony."

* * * * *

George's Sandwich Shop outdid its self with the preparation of Sue's reception. The back room was gleaming with new dazzling white linen, polished silver, and sparkling crystal. The florist had placed a long, low flower arrangement on the head table and small similar ones on each guest table. An open bar and bartender occupied a small alcove in the back.

The guests filled the room, happily conversing and imbibing. The wedding couple arrived with the photographer and slowly moved about the room. Pete did most of the introductions. Sue was aglow with her love for Pete. They made a beautiful couple.

"Patrick, Sue is so happy she's almost giddy."

"Yes, she is."

Millie walked up to Patrick and Laura and offered her hand to Patrick. "I understand congratulations are in order. You two will be getting married in October."

"Yes, thank you, Millie. I see you have met my fiancée."

"Yes, we met in the anteroom with Sue, just before the wedding."

"May I offer you our congratulations on your upcoming new member of your family."

"Millie's eyes lit with excitement. "Thank you. It's a boy. Bob is thrilled and so are my parents."

"How are Mr. and Mrs. Coger? Is your father still in advertising?"

"They're both fine, and, yes, he still has the company in Columbia."

"I'll have to get in touch with him, again."

Millie stiffened remembering how, last time, he withdrew his business from her father's agency. Then she relaxed realizing how the situation has changed.

"I'm sure he would appreciate it. They're here, now."

"Not today. I'll catch him at his office, soon."

After Millie left, Patrick and Laura sat at their assigned table. They were not there long before Sue was leading an attractive black woman and a tall, well-built man with skin the color of coffee.

"Laura, Patrick, this is Joellyn and Charles Godwin."

Patrick stood. "Charles, good to see you again."

The tall black man smiled revealing white even teeth.

"You know the Godwins?"

"Yes, Sue, Charles and I both serve on the county council. But I haven't had the pleasure of meeting Mrs. Godwin." Patrick extended his hand.

Joellyn smiled, and Laura couldn't help but think how beautiful their teeth were. A toothpaste ad.

Patrick put his hand on Charles Godwin's arm. "By any chance, did you have a visitor for a few days? One from New York?"

Godwin chuckled. "Guess you figured I was the Nam buddy who put up Roger Jackson. Dodge and I go back a few years."

"*Dodge?*"

"Carry-over from Nam. Roger-Dodger."

Patrick nodded. "I'll have to remember that."

Laura noticed Millie Sutherland and Joellyn Godwin were laughing and hugging each other and, going by the hands on the tummy, assumed they were talking about Millie's pregnancy. She later found out that Joellyn Godwin was pregnant, too. She wondered if she and Patrick would have a baby.

Caper Morgan walked up to Millie Sutherland and hugged her. She cocked her head to listen to what Millie was saying and then hugged her again. Caper crossed the room and came up to Laura.

"One of these days you'll have to tell me about Clark being in your bedroom."

"How did you know that?"

"Word travels. Anyway, we've got to get together for lunch at the club. Also, I have a few pictures of wedding gowns to show you. Let's do it soon."

"I'll make it a priority."

Caper Morgan turned and joined other townspeople. Laura watched the elegantly dressed woman move about the room. *Good for business.*

The afternoon was spent meeting neighbors and friends. A light repast was served and finally Sue and Pete left, under a gale of birdseed. Their honeymoon destination known only to themselves.

* * * * *

At home, Laura looked at her calendar. This coming Saturday would be Fourth of July. Kevin would be coming down from New York. Her nervousness became apparent by her trembling hands.

On Tuesday Patrick called. "I haven't heard from you since the wedding. Are you all right?"

"Yes, yes, of course. I was tied up with wedding plans."

"Good! What say we take a ride to Greenwood and have lunch at *Inn on the Square*?"

"Oh, I don't know, Patrick. I'm not too hungry."

"You sound so far off. Are you having misgivings about our wedding?"

"No!" Her voice sounded so sharp she caught her breath. "I didn't mean to sound so intense. I'm just a little nervous."

"Well, don't you get cold feet. I'd have to drag you before the preacher and Reverend Nicholson might not understand."

Laura chuckled visualizing the scene.

"That's my girl. I think I'll come over to keep you company."

Laura's spirit lifted. "Yes, Patrick. That would be wonderful."

* * * * *

"When did you say Kevin would arrive?"

Patrick felt the nervous vibe in Laura's hand. "Don't tell me you're nervous because Kevin is coming."

"Well, Patrick, I do so want him to like me. I have no experience with teenagers and I might not come up to his expectations."

"*Expectations!* He's not the one who is marrying you. I am. Kevin is an 'all right' kid. And besides, I can't imagine him not liking you."

"It's easy for you to say but I'm sure you can understand my qualms."

"Just remember one thing, Laura, you're not marrying the family, you're marrying me. And if my choice of a wife does not suit him, so be it, but it will have no effect upon our marriage. He has his life to live, I have mine." He picked up Laura's hand and kissed her palm. "Now, how about we go out for lunch?"

Laura smiled and sighed with relief. "I'll get my jacket."

CHAPTER 20

Kevin stood before his father in the foyer and Laura noticed he was as tall as Patrick. He had the same unruly lock of hair that Laura loved. His eyes were steely gray and his smile was beguiling. She thought him just as handsome as Patrick.

He's going to be a heart-breaker.

He turned to Laura and took her hand. "I have to commend you. Anyone who can put up with my father must be on the side of angels." He brushed a kiss on her cheek.

"I see the Irish blarney runs in the family."

"Indeed it does. Speaking about blarney, where is Blarney?"

With that, the kitchen door opened and Blarney came bouncing into the foyer. Robert had waited for the cue. The dog danced around the young man and Laura noticed the dog's eyes were indeed smiling.

Kevin extended his hand to Robert and shook it firmly. "Where is Mrs. Taylor?"

"She's in the kitchen fixin' your favorite dinner."

Kevin headed for the kitchen and in a moment Laura could hear the eerie sound of Mrs. Taylor's unheard response.

Patrick grinned. "He's probably twirling her around the kitchen. She adores him."

Laura relaxed. All of her nervousness vanished. She felt completely at home.

At home. Yes, this was her home. She felt she would be very happy living in Moultrie, South Carolina. The people were so friendly. But then, again, she knew she would be happy living anywhere with Patrick.

* * * * *

The October 12th issue of the *Moultrie Monitor* displayed a full page picture of Laura, and the article read:

On October 10, 1994, Miss Laura Crowder, formerly of Baxter's Mill, Richmond, Virginia, became the wife of Mr. Patrick Ryan of ERIN, Moultrie, South Carolina, at Holy Redeemer Church. The Reverend Nicholson officiated.

The bride was escorted in marriage by her half-brother, Mr. Peter Harris. She wore a shimmering gown of white satin trimmed in seed pearls, a finger-tip veil fell from a crown of seed pearls, and she carried six long stemmed calla lilies tied with satin ribbons.

Her matron-of-honor was Mrs. Peter Harris, who wore a bright rust colored gown and carried a nosegay of chrysanthemums of the same fall color.

Mr. Ryan's best man was his son Kevin Ryan of New York City.

An expansive reception was held at the Moultrie Country Club and was attended by a great number of Moultrie residents and distinguished out-of-town guests from New York City.

Mr. and Mrs. Patrick Ryan announced their honeymoon plans to go to New York City where they will attend a recital to be given by Kevin Ryan, son of Patrick Ryan, who is a student of music at the Juillard School, a prestigious college, and then continue on to "paradise" as Mr. Ryan stated.

The couple will return to Moultrie sometime in November where they will reside at ERIN.

* * * * *

On the way to the JFK airport, Patrick handed Laura an envelope.

With a questioning look, she opened it and frowned. "What's this, Patrick?"

"My wedding gift to you. It's a bank's transfer of funds. This week I had my accountant transfer a million dollars to an account in your name. I told you my offer was firm. Consider it a reverse dowry."